"You're funny, you know that?" He leaned against the open door, shaking his head. "How come you're not afraid of me?"

"Afraid of you? I'll give you 'afraid'!" She grabbed the nearest plastic bag stuffed with B.J.'s old junk and hurled it down the attic stairs. "You think I should be afraid of you?" She picked up a handful of old motorcycle magazines and threw them after it. "I'll show you who's afraid of you, you arrogant piece of toe-jam," she shrieked.

The sudden feeling of his arm around her surprised her more than anything else. Not just because she hadn't expected it, but because he felt so real . . . so close . . . so . . .

He lifted her off the ground as though it were she who was nothing.

"Put me down!" she screamed. "This minute! I mean it. Put me down!"

He dropped her on top of a filthy pile of old comics.

The laughter stopped. "Let's just get one thing straight here, princess. This is my home, and I ain't goin' nowhere."

You Can Never Go Home Again

Dyan Sheldon

Troll Associates

For Mike Fiorella,
and with special thanks to Bobbie.

This edition published in 2001.

Copyright © 1993 by Dyan Sheldon.

Published by Troll Associates, Inc.
WestWind is a trademark of Troll Associates.

First published in the United Kingdom by Bantam Books.

Cover design by Tony Greco & Associates.

Printed in the United States of America.

10 9 8 7 6 5 4 3 2

Chapter 1
Mama Said There'd Be Days Like This

Angel Lister stared glumly out the window as the BMW sped along. No matter what happened in the future—wars, famines, the return of the bubonic plague—she knew that this day would go down in history as the very worst day of Angel Lister's life.

The car turned onto a road lined with shopping centers and gas stations. She could feel her mother glancing over at her, but she didn't look around. Instead, she sighed heavily. She'd been sighing heavily since they'd left New Jersey, when she'd decided not to say another word. It was the quietest she'd been in months.

Ever since Angel's parents had decided to divorce and her mother had announced that she was taking Angel and her brother, Sean, to live on Long Island, Angel had done nothing but argue, complain, and cry. Even this morning, while the movers hauled their possessions out to the truck, Angel had sat on a box in the empty kitchen, crying. Later, while her mother piled things onto the roof of the car—so it looked like it belonged to a family of hillbillies—Angel had stood at the side door, arguing that she wasn't going and that there was no way Denise could make her go. And much later, when they were on the road and her brother was chattering in the backseat and her mother was singing along with the radio, Angel had gone through all her complaints about the move again. She'd given up when they'd entered New York State. She might never speak again.

"Look!" Denise suddenly cried.

Angel looked. Her mother was pointing to the town sign. Maybe she *would* speak again, after all. "'Welcome to Midville,'" she read sourly. And then added, "Cretin Capital of the World."

"That'll be enough of that," her mother said. Denise reached over and patted Angel's knee. "Honey, I know this is a big change, but you have to give it a chance. You just wait and see. We're starting all over, and it's going to be great."

Angel sighed again. That was easy for her mother to say. Denise wanted to start all over. She wanted to give up her comfortable life and run a diner. But Angel didn't want to give up her comfortable life to be the daughter of a waitress. She didn't want to live on Long Island. She wanted to stay in Maryland, in their beautiful home in Lisson Park, with its Jacuzzi, its bathroom off every bedroom, and its swimming pool in the backyard. She wanted to stay where everybody knew her and admired her. In Lisson Park, she went out with Gavin Spencer Smythe, the handsomest and most popular boy in her exclusive private school. In Lisson Park, she and her best friend, Lindy Porterfield, were the campus trendsetters and cocaptains of the cheerleaders. Nothing of any importance happened in Lisson Park without Angel Lister. But in Midville, Long Island, Angel knew no one. She had to go to a public school. She wouldn't even have her own phone, never mind her own bathroom. The only glimmer of light in the whole black nightmare was the fact that the new house was by the beach. Having a beach in your backyard was even—marginally—better than having a pool. Every once in awhile, when she managed to forget her misery for a second or two, Angel imagined having parties there. She could hear herself saying to her friends—friends who looked amazingly like her friends back in Lisson Park—"Hey, why don't you come over to my beach on Saturday? We can have a barbecue."

Sean, who had been dozing for the last half hour, woke up. "Are we there?" He rubbed his eyes. "Where's our house?"

Denise laughed. "We're not there yet, but we're close," she said. "Keep your eyes peeled. See if you can tell which one is ours."

They passed a row of attractive, modern houses with satellite dishes; large, well kept lawns; and new cars in their broad driveways. Angel sat up a little straighter. *Maybe this isn't going to be so bad after all,* she thought. *It isn't Lisson Park, but it's livable.*

Sean pointed to a sprawling brick ranch house with a row of brightly colored windsocks hanging from its porch. "That one!" he screamed. "That's our house!"

Angel held her breath, willing her mother to say yes. The ranch was smaller than their old house, but it did have a swimming pool and a two-car garage. Angel could imagine her friends coming up the flag-stone walk, past the neatly trimmed hedges. She could hear herself saying to Lindy, "It's actually not so bad. My room has real wooden shutters and everything."

Denise said no.

"Oh, no." Denise sounded almost as though she had considered the ranch house but had rejected it as not quite good enough. "Ours has a lot more character than that." She waved one hand dismissively. "And besides, ours is on the beach."

They turned off the main road and started up a steep hill. Angel started looking for a house with a lot of character and a beach behind it, hope bleeping in her heart. The farther they went, however, the smaller, older, and closer together the houses became. There were toys on the grass and junk on the porches. The screens were torn, and the paint was peeling. Hope's bleeping became fainter and fainter.

"Are you sure this is right?" asked Angel. "Maybe we're going in the wrong direction."

"This is right," said Denise. "Can't you smell the water?"

Sean stuck his head out the window. "I can!" he shouted. "I can smell the ocean!"

Angel groaned but kept her eyes on the street signs: Gull Court, Shore Road, Sandy Street. At least there really was a beach. "It's not the ocean, stupid," she yelled over her shoulder. "It's the Sound."

Sean kicked the back of Angel's seat. "You're stupid."

"It's not much farther," Denise announced brightly. "Just a few more blocks."

A few more blocks into hell, thought Angel, her heart sinking deeper with each passing street. This was like something out of a black-and-white movie. One of those dumb black-and-white movies in which everyone is unhappy and the hero dies at the

8

end in either a gang fight or a car crash.

She wrinkled her nose in disgust. All the children looked dirty. Middle-aged women—women wearing old clothes and no makeup—were mowing lawns. Every other driveway had some man lying on his back under a rusty old car. Angel's father, Marshall, could hardly change a lightbulb, never mind repair his Mercedes. In Lisson Park, everyone had gardeners to tend their lawns and mechanics to fix their cars. In Lisson Park, the children were clean and the women never left their homes if they didn't look as though they were about to be photographed.

They passed two houses painted the same unlikely shade of electric blue. *This is not Lisson Park,* Angel reminded herself. If anything, it was like an amusement park. This was a place where people kept bathtubs full of dead geraniums and trailers in their yards and painted their homes to look like fun houses.

Angel couldn't stand much more. She closed her eyes.

The BMW turned left. "We're almost there," said Denise, her voice excited. "Number 52, Bluff Drive, coming up!"

In Lisson Park, the houses had names, not just numbers. Names like Silver Knoll or Beecham or Windy Point. What could you call these houses? Bikes on the Grass? Weedview? Blue Nightmare?

The car stopped.

"This is it!" cried Denise. "Isn't it terrific?"

Be brave, Angel told herself. *Remember the beach. Remember it's got character.* She opened her eyes.

The moving van was in the driveway, and their sofa was just disappearing through the front door. Her mother was already out of the car, gazing at 52 Bluff Drive as though she'd never seen anything like it before. Sean scrambled after her, carrying his gerbil's cage.

"Wow!" he shrieked. "This is really neat!" He held up the cage. "Look, Germy, isn't this neat?"

Angel didn't know what Germy's response was, but she said nothing herself. She couldn't. She couldn't speak. Angel had never seen anything quite like this before, either.

Number 52, Bluff Drive was a small, two-story wooden building surrounded by half-wild trees and shrubs and foot-high crabgrass and weeds. Its dirty white paint was peeling, its tiny porch was sagging, its windows were warped and filthy, its few remaining shutters were broken, and the garage had only half a door. Any character it had was all bad.

This has to be a joke, Angel told herself. *My mother can't really expect me to live here.*

But, of course, her mother *did* expect her to live here. Even as she sat there, staring at the house in disbelief, one of the movers disappeared through the front door with Angel's armchair over his head.

Denise turned toward the car. "Come on out here, honey!" she called. "Come see!"

I've seen enough, Angel thought, but she slowly climbed out anyway. Maybe the back of the house looked different. Better. That was where the sliding glass doors must be. The sliding glass doors that lead to the beach.

"That's your room, up at the front," Denise was saying to Sean. She pointed to an almost black square of what must be glass on the second floor. "There's a

10

little recess in the roof right outside your window where you can sit."

Sean started jumping up and down. "That's perfect, Mom! That's perfect! I can put my telescope out there and everything." He placed the gerbil cage on the ground. "Mind Germy," he ordered. "I'm going to explore."

"And that's your room," Denise was now saying. She gestured toward a microscopic window at the side of the porch. One of the panes was cracked. "It's not very big, but it gives you plenty of privacy."

No private bathroom, no private telephone, no wall-to-wall carpets, no Jacuzzi, no space, but plenty of privacy. Just like solitary confinement. At last Angel recovered the power of speech. "Just how big is not very big?" she asked.

Denise went on as though Angel hadn't spoken. "Once it's painted, it'll be very cozy." She smiled at Angel in a way that suggested that this information should make her happy.

Angel didn't return her mother's smile. "And who's going to paint it?"

Denise laughed. "Why, *you* are, of course." She put her arm around Angel's shoulder. "Come on. I'll show you the beach."

Denise showed Angel the beach. There were no sliding glass doors. There was no strip of soft sand leading from the patio to the clear blue water of the Sound. *Well, what did you expect?* she asked herself. *A real beach? A real beach with real cabanas and a real snack bar? With regular people having fun?*

"You better hold onto that tree," Denise warned. "You don't want to slip."

11

At least if I slipped, I wouldn't have to live here, thought Angel, but she grabbed onto the tree just the same. If she was going to die, she wanted to die slowly, of misery, so that her mother would be racked with guilt.

"Just look at that!" said Denise. "Isn't it fantastic?"

Angel looked. Sixty feet below them, straight down a rocky bluff, was the narrow, deserted beach. Seagulls picked their way among the rubble and shells. The water was brown, the tide was low, and a few yards from the shoreline two enormous black boulders poked from the water like stranded whales. Even from up here, Angel could smell dead fish and seaweed.

Denise sighed. "Well," she prodded. "Isn't it breathtaking?"

Angel nodded. It certainly was taking her breath away. "How do we get down there?" she asked. "Jump?"

"There's a public staircase along here somewhere." Denise waved vaguely toward the left, but her eyes were still on the horizon. "You know," she said in a far-away voice, "I already feel like a different person. . . ."

Angel was about to say that, as far as she was concerned, Denise *was* a different person—the mother from *The Twilight Zone*—when Sean came racing up to them, jabbering away, and cut her off.

"There's all this stuff in the garage . . . and there's a great place for a tree house . . . and wait'll you see inside. I couldn't look around much because of the movers, but it looks really cool. . . ." He was so excited that he couldn't stand still. "It's just like we lived in an old castle or something. You know, like in a movie. I bet spies or vampires used to live here. I bet somebody was murdered in the house." He bounced up and down, tugging on Denise's arm. "Wouldn't that be great, Mom? Maybe in my room, even. Maybe someone was stabbed in my room! Maybe you can still see the bloodstains!"

Castle? How could he compare this disgusting, rotten little cottage to a castle? Angel looked down at her brother. Then, again, how could this peculiar child possibly be a relative of *hers*? "Maybe you'll be stabbed in your room," she said sweetly.

But Sean didn't hear her. He was already rushing off in another direction. "I'm going to check out the beach," he called. "I'll be back soon."

"Be careful!" Denise shouted after him. "Don't go too far!" She turned to Angel with a smile. "Well?" she asked, putting a hand on her shoulder. "Sean's thrilled. And I'm thrilled. What about you? What do you think of our new home?"

Angel couldn't believe her mother actually had to ask. "Think?" she screeched. "What do I *think*? I think you're both out of your minds, that's what I think!" She started shaking uncontrollably. "This is the worst hole I've ever seen in my life. You couldn't pay rats to live here."

Denise gave her a shake. "Oh, come on, honey," she said soothingly. "I know this is difficult for you, it's all been so rushed and everything . . . but I do think you're overreacting. You're tired now. Trust me, it'll all look better in the morning."

It seemed impossible that anyone who had cried as much as Angel had in the past few weeks could have any tears left, but, amazingly enough, she felt them welling up in her. "It'll never look better!" she

13

screamed, breaking free from her mother. "Not unless it's blown up!"

The movers began carrying things upstairs. As their footsteps and voices reached the second-floor landing, something—someone—stirred in the bedroom that faced the street. Just a slight movement. Just a shifting in the shadows. Just a sudden draft in the corner. From behind the dirt-encrusted window, his dark, depthless eyes had seen everything, but now he turned back to the room—listening, watching the door.

These people always made him want to laugh. He heard them talking about where to put the sofa and what curtains to hang in the kitchen and who was going to sleep where, and it made him want to roar with laughter. *You wish!* he wanted to tell them. *Dream on! Like you're really gonna stay. Like this is gonna be your nice, safe little home.*

Laugh? It cracked him up. *Don't bother unpacking,* he felt like saying. *Don't start puttin' up your pictures and painting the walls. Take it from me, you're wastin' your time.*

He'd seen it all a hundred times before. Or at least fifty or sixty. After thirty-plus years, it was easy to lose count. They moved in; they moved out. Maybe they got all their stuff unpacked; maybe they only had time for a cup of instant coffee and a Twinkie. Sometimes he thought he should just meet them at the door. He should be standing there when they arrived, smiling like a good host. "Do yourself a favor," he'd tell them. "Get out of here now." But that would be too easy. That wouldn't be any fun. And, anyway, he didn't want them to see or hear him. He didn't want them interested or curious. He just wanted them scared. Scared, and screaming, and gone—one way or another. *You've got a choice,* he could tell them. *Fast and easy, or slow and hard.*

Usually, it was easy. All it took was a little noise in the night, a few unexpected occurrences, a couple of unexplained events. People didn't like hearing things they couldn't see or seeing things that shouldn't be there. People didn't like inconvenience. They were squeamish about terror.

Something heavy thudded against the door. "Yo, Mike!" said a voice on the other side. "Give me a hand, will ya? It's stuck or somethin'."

A smile as dark as those eyes appeared on his face. He crossed the room. This time, he knew, it was going to be very easy. What could be easier than a woman, a girl, and a small boy? Easy and fast. He wouldn't be surprised if they didn't last the night.

There were a few more thuds, and then the doorknob turned several times. Of course, nothing happened.

"It's not stuck," said another voice. "It's locked."

"Locked?" The first mover laughed. "It can't be locked. There ain't no keyhole."

The one named Mike rattled the knob again. "Then it's locked from the inside, isn't it, Einstein?"

The first mover laughed again. "From the *inside*? Stupid, if it was locked from the inside, there'd hafta be somebody in there, and there ain't been anyone in this place for years." He threw himself against the door again. "Come on, Mike," he urged. "One more time. On the count of three."

The eyes unblinking, the lips still smiling, he slowly put his hand on the knob.

"One . . . two . . ."

Let the fun begin! he said to himself.

"Three—"

He jerked the door open so quickly that the movers didn't come to a stop until they hit the opposite wall.

Laugh? He could die laughing.

If he weren't dead already.

Chapter 2

Shake, Rattle, and Roll

The first thing Angel heard the next morning was her mother's voice shouting, "Angel! Sean! It's about time the two of you got up!" The house was so small that Denise sounded as though she were in the same room. The kitchen door slammed, and the wall beside Angel's bed shook. She opened her eyes.

A large water stain, shaped remarkably like Long Island itself, stretched across the ceiling over Angel's bed. A bare light bulb, peppered with dead insects, hung beside it. Her eyes moved down. The walls were papered in white carnations on a field of forest green. Her stylish, expensive furniture—or the few pieces of her stylish, expensive furniture that the movers had managed to cram into the minute room—looked as out of place in the tasteless gloom as a diamond necklace worn with a flannel shirt. Angel groaned out loud. Her mother was wrong again. Nothing looked better in the morning.

Since no room in this house was very far away from any other, Angel could hear Denise thumping around in the kitchen. She sighed. Although she and her mother hadn't actually been speaking last night, Denise had nonetheless made it clear that she expected Angel to help with the unpacking today. Angel kicked off the covers. Which meant that her nails would be ruined and her hair would go frizzy with sweat. Not, of course, that her mother would care.

Resigned to her unhappy fate, Angel sat up. The only advantage of living in a room the size of a cracker box was that she could see herself in the mirror of her dressing table without having to get out of bed. She looked awful. Because the old house creaked and groaned so much, it had taken her hours to get to sleep last night, and now there were dark circles under her eyes. She stared at her reflection. Actually, the effect wasn't that bad. She definitely looked like she was suffering. Angel tilted her head first one way then the other. Yes, she looked like a beautiful young girl whose cruel mother had torn her away from everyone and everything she loved best. Which, of course, she was. Angel struck a tragic pose. No one could see that face and not realize she was pining away from a broken heart.

Apparently her mother could see Angel's face and not realize she was pining away from a broken heart. "Sleep all right?" Denise asked coldly as Angel came into the kitchen.

"I may never sleep again," said Angel as she flung herself into the nearest chair. "Not in this house."

Denise set a pitcher of juice in the center of the table. "And how are we feeling this morning?" she asked, her voice still the temperature of an Alaskan winter. "Semihuman?"

Angel reached for the juice. She could tell that her mother wanted to clear the air after their fight—and, to be honest, part of her wanted to clear the air, too. But for some reason Angel always hated to be the one to give in. Lindy said it was because she was as stubborn as a team of mules, but Angel was sure it wasn't that. She wasn't stubborn; it was just that she was usually right. "Semihuman is about all you could feel in this dump," Angel grumbled.

Denise leaned back against the old wooden counter. She was wearing her no-nonsense expression. "Look," she said, "I know you're upset, Angel, but I do think you owe me an apology for the way you behaved yesterday."

Angel drew a circle in the moisture on the outside of the pitcher. She supposed that, if she were being honest with herself, she would admit that her mother was right about that, as well. She probably *did* owe Denise an apology. A small one. Not only had Angel stormed off in a temper, but she'd locked herself in the car and refused to come out until Denise threatened to have one of the movers drag her out. "I just don't understand why you didn't rent a real house, that's all," she said at last. "They have real houses on Long Island. We passed some on the way."

Her mother made a sound Angel recognized as the sigh of a woman who had explained something a dozen times and can't believe she has to explain it again. Mademoiselle Baget, Angel's French teacher, had sighed in exactly the same way when she'd tried to make Angel understand the subjunctive mood with French verbs.

"I've told you," said Denise. "Because this is the house we could afford. You know I needed all the money from the sale of Silver Knoll for the restaurant.

I've put every cent I have into that."

Angel knew. She'd have to be deaf and in Argentina not to know. The diner was her mother's grand plan. Denise had wanted to have something she could make a living at that gave her a new focus for herself at the same time. Not just a job, she'd said over and over, but a whole new life.

"This isn't easy for me, either, you know," Denise added in almost a whisper.

There was something in her mother's voice that caught Angel's attention. She glanced over. Denise looked almost as though she might cry herself. In spite of Angel's own suffering, a sudden rush of feeling for her mother overcame her. She smiled sympathetically. "It's not a restaurant," she teased. "It's a diner."

Denise laughed. "But it's a very good diner." She leaned over and brushed a strand of hair from Angel's eyes, just as she'd done when Angel was little. "And it'll be a lot better by the time I get done with it."

Angel wasn't sure whether she was actually going to say the words "I'm sorry" to her mother out loud or not, but, at that moment, the kitchen door was flung open and Sean more or less threw himself into the room.

He really is the weirdest little kid, thought Angel as she watched her brother land in a chair. His shirt was inside out, and his hair was sticking straight up. The bridge of his glasses was held together with adhesive tape. He was so excited, he was babbling.

"I knew it! I knew this was like a vampire's castle! I knew someone must've been killed here!" He knocked the cereal box over.

Denise paused in the act of putting bread into the

toaster. "What happened to your glasses?" she demanded.

Sean, as usual, wasn't listening. "But didn't you hear it, Mom? Didn't you hear all those noises last night?"

"Your glasses, Sean," Denise said. "What happened to them?"

"They fell off when I was looking for the blood."

Angel looked at her mother. Denise was looking at Sean. Sean went on as though breaking your glasses while looking for blood was the most normal thing in the world. "But you didn't?" he persisted. "Didn't you hear all the noise?"

Denise gave up with a shrug. "I didn't hear anything," she said, going back to the toast. "I was asleep as soon as I closed my eyes."

Sean turned to Angel, sweeping his spoon off the table. "But you heard it, didn't you, Angel? You must've heard it. There was all this thudding and running and somebody punching the walls. . . ." He knocked the butter dish into the juice.

Denise put a hand on his shoulder. "Take it easy, will you, Sean? You're going to destroy the place before we're unpacked."

Angel rolled her eyes. It amazed her that her mother could be so tolerant of Sean. She actually talked to him as though she thought he were human. "I heard a lot of noise," said Angel, moving the pitcher out of Sean's range. "But it wasn't anybody punching the walls. It was just the house falling down."

"No, you're wrong, you're wrong." Sean shook his head so hard his glasses slid off. "Look, I wrote it all down." He pulled a chewed-looking piece of loose-leaf paper from his pocket. "At ten, the thumping started. I couldn't really tell where it was coming from, though. It kept moving around. Then it stopped for awhile, but it started again around eleven. Then I heard someone hitting something. You know, a wall or something. And then, just as I was falling asleep, I heard someone running down the stairs, but when I went to look, there was nobody there."

"You mean there's nobody there," said Angel, tapping his head.

Sean ignored her, his eyes on his notes. "And then, around one, the dog started crying. It was really sad." He looked from his mother to his sister, his expression anything but sad. "Isn't it great?" he demanded. "It's even better than vampires. We have a ghost!"

Denise put a hand on his forehead. "You're not coming down with something, are you?"

Angel passed him the milk. "Well, find out where your ghost is staying, and maybe we can swap rooms. The only person who could live in mine is someone without a body."

Sean took the container from her, pouring almost as much on the table as in his bowl. "Ghosts don't have rooms," he informed her. "They just drift around."

Angel passed him a wad of napkins. "I'm going to start drifting around, too." She gave her mother a pointed look. "I'm afraid to sleep in my room. It's so small I might suffocate during the night."

Sean started shoveling cereal into his face. "So why don't you sleep in the attic, then?" he mumbled between mouthfuls.

Angel watched milk and cornflakes dribble down her brother's chin. She couldn't possibly have heard him right. "What?"

"The attic," he mumbled again. "If your room's so small, maybe you could sleep in the attic. It's bound to be bigger."

A rare but genuine feeling of affection for her baby brother overtook her. What a clever little boy he was to think of the attic. And thoughtful. Thoughtful to suggest it. "Really?" she asked. "Have you been up there? How big is it?"

Sean shook his head. "I only saw it from outside." He wiped his mouth with the back of his sleeve. "Yesterday. When I was looking around."

It'd been so long since she'd felt anything but miserable that it was hard for Angel to tell if what was racing through her heart was excitement or not. But an attic: Sean was right, even an attic had to be better than what she had now. The Porterfields' maid slept in their attic, and her room was five times the size of Angel's.

"There is no attic," Denise said simply. "The realtor would have shown it to me." She put a plate of toast on the table and took her seat between them.

"No, there is, Mom, really." Sean reached for the toast. "You can see the window from the back of the house, facing the water."

Denise gently removed his sleeve from the butter. "I'm sure it isn't any more than a storage space," she said. "You know, for screens and stuff like that." She took a sip of coffee. "And, anyway, we have enough to do cleaning up the rest of the house without either of you wasting time crawling around up there."

23

Angel pushed her plate away with a sigh. *I should have known,* she thought, her few seconds of hope gone, just as though they had never happened. *A storage attic. With my luck, it couldn't be anything else.*

They were leaving. He could hear them downstairs, opening closets and turning off switches. He could hear them talking. He stood at the window of the boy's room, willing them to go; to go and not return. *Just get in your fancy car and go back where you came from. Get out of my house and leave me alone.*

"Come on, you two," the woman was shouting. "Midville awaits!"

Someone groaned.

When he heard the front door open and shut, he carefully moved the curtain aside. Someone had cleaned the window since yesterday. He squinted in the unaccustomed light. The world outside looked different somehow. It had been a long, long time since he'd seen it other than through a dull film of dirt. He'd forgotten how green the trees were and how even the road seemed to shine in the sun.

The mother led the way to the car, followed by the boy and then the girl. "Are you ready for the grand tour?" the woman asked. The car keys jangled in her hand.

"This should take all of five minutes," said the girl. She kicked a stone across the lawn.

Halfway down the path, for no apparent reason, the boy suddenly stopped.

"Keep going," he whispered. "That's a good boy. Get in the car."

But he wasn't a good boy. He didn't keep going;

24

he didn't get in the car. Instead, he turned around, almost as though he'd heard his name called. The boy's eyes went straight to the bedroom window—straight to him.

"Sean!" his mother yelled. "Sean! What are you doing? Come on!"

The boy—Sean—shielded his eyes with his hand. "Just a minute, Mom. I think I see something."

He watched the boy's expression change from puzzlement to certainty.

All at once, the boy started shouting. "I *do!*" he cried. "I do see something! There's somebody watching us from my window! There's somebody there!"

He was too surprised to drop the curtain and step back. The boy shouldn't be able to see him when he hadn't materialized. No one ever had before. They saw the things he moved, but he could walk up and stare a person in the face and not be seen. They heard the noises he made, but he could shout in someone's ear and they wouldn't hear a thing.

The girl didn't bother to look. "You really are too weird to live," she said as she stalked past her brother.

The mother was unlocking the car. "Sean, please." She shook her head. "I wish I knew where you got that imagination from."

The boy, Sean, was still staring right at him. Nothing like this had ever happened before. He could see him squinting behind the broken round glasses. He could see the look of concentration on his face. He wished he could make himself vanish, and he wished he knew why the boy could see him. This wasn't the way things were supposed to work. None of it was. Last night should have been enough. After

25

the racket he'd made, they should all have been up and packing and ready to leave by dawn. But the only one who'd taken the slightest notice was the boy. And he hadn't been afraid. He'd come tiptoeing into the hallway after him. "Mr. Ghost? Mr. Ghost?" he'd called. "Mr. Ghost, where are you?"

"It's not my imagination!" the boy was shouting. "There's someone in my room. Can't you see him? He's at the left of the window. He looks really strange."

The girl spun around. "Oh, sure," she said. "Like the time you saw a spaceship land in Washington through your binoculars."

"It's not binoculars." He took a few more steps toward the house. "It's a telescope."

His sister went after him. "Some jerk," she said. It was the first time he'd heard her laugh. "I can't believe you really called the FBI."

"Sean!" The mother started the engine. "Sean, I want you in this car this minute."

The boy didn't move.

And he didn't move.

"Okay," the boy was saying, "so I made a mistake about the spaceship. But this time I'm right. I *know* I'm right." The boy pointed at the window, to exactly the spot where his heart had been. "Look up there!" he ordered. "There's somebody in my room! You can see him!"

This time, the girl looked. She yawned. "There's nothing there, ant-brain. You didn't shut the curtain right, that's all." She grabbed hold of her brother's arm. "Come on, Mr. Weirdest, before the little green men come to get you."

Reluctantly, his eyes still on him, the boy let himself be led away. "He's not green," he protested. "And he's not little. He's enormous."

The mother was staring at the window. "He's not anything," she said. "He's a trick of light."

"Trick of light," he repeated as the car pulled away. "We'll see about that."

As soon as they turned down Main Street, Denise started pointing things out as though they really were on a grand tour. "That's the church I went to when I was a kid," she announced, nodding to the left. She nodded to the right. "That's where Sally, my best friend in elementary school, used to live." She gestured to a white brick building. "And that's the office of the real estate agent who rented us the house," she said.

"Good, let's bomb it," Angel snarled from the passenger seat. It was almost pathetic, she decided as they crawled the few blocks that made up the town. Here her mother was all excited about showing them Midville, and there was nothing to see. No movie house. No pizzeria. No video store. No health club. No jewelry boutique. There was only one clothing shop, and Angel could tell at a glance that no one under thirty would be caught dead buying anything in it. She leaned her head against the window. Her friends in Lisson Park had tried to tell her that Midville couldn't possibly be as bad as she imagined, but her friends had been wrong. It was worse. They might as well have moved to the moon. If they had, at least she'd have gotten her picture in the papers.

"Look over there," Denise said, in the bright voice

of a guide. "That's the town newspaper. It's been going since 1804. Isn't that something? And that deli next to it used to be the candy store where we hung out when I was a teenager."

Sean threw himself against the front seat. "Hey!" he shouted. "There's a fishing store!"

Angel gave him a swat without turning around. "What do you care? The only time you went fishing, you fainted."

Sean slapped her on the top of the head. "I thought Dad would like it, that's what. I was just wishing he could see it."

Denise steered into a parking space. "And here is the soon-to-be-famous Blue Moon Diner," she announced proudly. "Proprietor, your mother."

Even from the car they could hear the din of sawing, drilling, and hammering coming from inside.

Sean opened his door, banging it against the car in the next space. "Wow. Our own diner. This is really great!"

Denise grinned with pleasure. "As you can hear, the contractors are already hard at work. Everything's go!"

Angel scowled at the building in front of them. It vaguely resembled a railroad car in the same way that 52 Bluff Drive vaguely resembled a house. Except that the diner wasn't small and white and falling down. It was small and yellow and trimmed in chrome. It was exactly the kind of place moving men who wore earrings and bandannas went for lunch.

Denise was already on the curb with Sean, going on about what color she was having the diner painted and why she'd decided on a new front door. Angel had never seen her mother so thrilled about anything before. Not even when she'd been made chairperson of the country-club ball. Not even when her bowling team had made the league championships.

"I'm having a blue neon light in the shape of a crescent moon put on the roof," Denise was saying as Angel came up beside her. "And I thought that maybe, instead of curtains, I'd hang strands of silver stars in the windows."

"Oh, great," said Angel. "Then it won't look like a diner. It'll look like a gypsy tearoom."

Normally, her mother would have told her to watch it after a remark like that, but today she was in such a good mood that even sarcasm didn't bother her.

"Come on," she said, grabbing them both by the hand. "I want to show you inside."

"I'm going to have to take a nap when we get home," said Angel as she followed her mother through the chrome door. "To recover from all this excitement."

Angel had been wrong about one thing. There *was* a pizzeria, in the shopping center north of the town. Because she said they had too much to do to bother about cooking, Denise stopped to pick up a pie for lunch. "If this is good, we can go back and get heroes for supper," she said as she put her key in the lock.

Angel stood behind her, holding the pizza and trying to keep Sean from knocking it out of her hands. "Hurry up, Mom," she urged. "It's getting cold."

"All right, all right," said Denise. "Keep your shirt on." She pushed open the door. She caught her breath.

29

Sean shoved against Angel. "Mommm," she moaned when Denise didn't move. "What are you doing? Let's go in the house."

Her mother didn't answer. She just stood there in the doorway, as still as a stone.

Angel nudged her mother with the pizza box. "Mom . . ."

Denise still didn't move.

She nudged her again. "Mom . . ."

At last, Denise made a response. "Oh, my God," she said in a horrified whisper.

"Let me see," Sean said, pushing past her. "What's going on?"

"I don't believe this," Denise said, shaking her head back and forth. "I just don't believe this. Who could have— What—"

"Wow!" shrieked Sean. "This is great!"

Angel peered over her mother's shoulder. She caught her breath, just as Denise had. "Oh, my God! What's going on?"

It looked as though the house had been hit by a tornado. Or by an army of wild chimps. It looked as though everything they owned had been unpacked and strewn around the living room. Clothes were draped over the banister. Pots and pans hung from the walls. The lamps were draped with necklaces and earrings. Germy's cage swung from the ceiling light. Instead of wall-to-wall carpet, they had wall-to-wall *things*. Heaps of books and coats and magazines and pictures. Piles of dishes and linens and shoes.

Very slowly, Denise stepped into the room, Angel beside her.

"What do you think happened?" asked Angel softly.

30

Denise's eyes scanned the room, from the papers scattered all down the stairs to the blobs of shampoo and detergent dripping down the walls. "It must be burglars," she said at last. "We must have left a window open or something."

Sean was already dragging a stool into the center of the room. "It's not burglars," he said as he climbed up and reached from the gerbil's cage. "Didn't you guys see *Poltergeist*? It's the ghost!"

Chapter 3
In the Still
of the Night

"I think I must be losing my mind." Denise stood at the stove, gazing into the depths of a large blue pan with a puzzled expression on her face. "I was sure I'd turned the burner on under the sauce." She shook her head. "That's at least the fourth time I've done something like that today."

Angel didn't say anything. She was staring critically at her reflection in the mirror on the shelf over the kitchen sink. She no longer looked as though she were pining away from a broken heart. Her mother had made her work so hard in the last two days that she now looked as though she were about to drop dead from exhaustion.

"Angel!" Denise nudged her. "You're supposed to be making the salad, not admiring yourself in the mirror."

Angel picked up the lettuce with a sigh. "I wasn't admiring myself," she said. "I was looking for signs of premature aging."

Denise laughed ruefully. "It's a wonder we haven't all gone gray. All our things thrown around . . . dish detergent all over the walls . . . a hanging gerbil. . . . What a welcome!" She turned on the stove, putting her hand near the burner to feel the heat. Satisfied, she put the saucepan back in place. "Still, it was obviously just kids fooling around. Those new locks should keep them out from now on."

Angel gazed at her mother in astonishment. It wasn't just love that was blind, she decided. It was also middle-aged women who were starting all over. "Fooling around? Mom, nobody fools around like that in Lisson Park." She started shredding the leaves and tossing them into the salad spinner. "Those weren't kids who vandalized our things. Those were serious criminals."

Denise picked up a wooden spoon. "Oh, I can't believe that, honey. The place was vacant for some time, remember. That mess was probably made by a group who used to hang out here."

Angel made a face. "What I can't believe is that you intend to stay here after that. That's what I can't believe." She turned on the faucet. "What would Daddy say if he knew you were putting his children at risk?"

Denise pointed the spoon at Angel. "I'm not putting anybody's children at risk," she said firmly. "It was just a prank. There was no harm done." She gave the sauce a stir.

No harm done! That was rich! Angel's hands were red, her back hurt, and she was so tired at night that she barely had the energy to crawl into bed—and her mother said there was no harm done! "I know you don't care that I'm going to end up looking like a cleaning lady," said Angel, "but you must have noticed that the walls are ruined."

Denise smiled wryly. "They had to be painted anyway."

Angel made a face as she started to turn the spinner. "What do they have to do, start shooting at us?" she asked. Yesterday and today, while they cleaned and scrubbed and put things away, she had tried to convince her mother that what had happened was a sign that they shouldn't be here. But Denise was too pigheaded to listen to a word she said. "Mom, wake up and smell the coffee," Angel pleaded. "Can't you see that God's trying to tell us to go back to Maryland?" She dumped the washed lettuce into the bowl.

"God's not trying to tell us any such thing," Denise answered, tearing open a box of pasta shells. "This is my life. And if you think I'm giving up now, when I haven't even started, then you have another thing coming." She tossed the empty box into the garbage.

But what about my life? Angel raged to herself. *What about me?* She was about to ask her mother this question when the back door shot open and Sean exploded into the kitchen. She turned on him, glaring. "Why can't you ever just walk into a room like a normal person?" she demanded.

Sean skidded to a stop beside his mother. He grabbed her arm. "Wait'll you hear!" he shouted. His cheeks were flushed and his face was damp with sweat. "This is fantastic! This is the greatest, neatest, most mind-boggling thing you've ever heard!"

"Don't tell me," said Angel, banging the bowl of salad on the table. "You're running away from home."

"Wash up, honey," said Denise. "We're almost ready to eat."

34

"But wait'll you hear, Mom! Wait'll you hear!" Sean went on at full speed. "I met this old man down the street, Mr. Stucker? He lives in that sort of pink house with the trailer next to it? Mr. Stucker's lived here since 1960!"

"He deserves a medal," said Angel, putting out the pan of sauce.

Sean ignored her. "Mr. Stucker says everybody used to call this the Spatano place," he informed them. He waved his hands under the faucet and dried them on the dish towel. "Mr. Stucker says they were the people who used to live here."

Denise looked over her shoulder at him. "Really? Did Mr. Stucker know them? Were they the ones who built the house?"

Sean threw himself onto his chair. "Uh-uh. They built the house, but they moved out before Mr. Stucker came."

Denise looked thoughtful. "He must have known the people who bought it from them, though."

"No, he didn't know them, either. The people who bought it from the Spatanos left just when Mr. Stucker got here." Sean reached for the bread. "Mr. Stucker knew the people who bought it from them. But they only stayed a couple of months."

Angel sat down, looking from her mother to her brother in disbelief. Were they really having a serious conversation about who used to live *here*? Welcome to Midville, home of the hick.

"Mr. Stucker says that no one stays here for very long," Sean announced.

"Well, there's no big surprise about that," Angel remarked.

Denise frowned. "But that doesn't make any sense." She placed the pasta on the table and took her seat. "The real estate agent didn't say there were any problems with the house. She said I was lucky to get it so reasonably."

"Oh, give me a break, Mom," groaned Angel. "What did you *think* she'd say? That no one can stand to live here for more than a week?"

Sean started bouncing in his seat. "But that's what I'm trying to tell you!" he shrieked, spraying bits of bread across the table. "That's the incredible news!"

Denise touched his arm. "Calm down, honey. It can't be *that* incredible."

"What is it?" Angel asked. "That no one's stupid enough to live here but us?"

"Yes, that's almost right!" He was shaking his head so hard his glasses fell onto his plate. "But you have to guess why. That's the fantastic thing. Guess *why* no one wants to live here."

"I mean it, Sean," Denise warned. "You have to calm down. You know what happens when you get too excited. You'll make yourself sick."

Angel moaned. "Oh, God, do we have to talk about vomit while we're eating?"

"Because it's haunted!" Sean screamed. "I told you, didn't I? You wouldn't believe me, but I was right. It's because the house is haunted!" He beamed across the table at them. "Isn't that the most terrific thing you've ever heard? I was right. We live in a haunted house!"

Angel looked at Denise. Denise looked at Angel. At exactly the same second, they both burst out laughing.

"What's so funny?" Sean demanded. "It's true. It

36

really is haunted. Mr. Stucker said so. Just like in *Poltergeist!* Just like I said!"

"Well, that's good news," gasped Angel. "That means we should get back to Lisson Park before demons start puking all over the kitchen."

Sean kicked her under the table. "It's not demons, dummy. It's Billy Spatano. Mr. Stucker says that he's the reason the Spatanos left Midville in a hurry. Because Billy died. Mr. Stucker said there was a big scandal and—"

Denise cut him off. "Sean," she said reasonably, "you know as well as we do that there's no such thing as ghosts."

"But there is!" Sean leaned forward urgently. "Didn't I tell you I heard stuff last night and the night before? It was the ghost! Didn't I tell you it was the ghost?"

Angel threw a pasta shell at him. "Didn't I tell you you were adopted? Mom and Dad only took you in because they felt sorry for you."

Sean's voice went into whine. "But it is true. That's why no one can live here. And Mr. Stucker says the whole block hears a dog howling whenever it storms."

Denise piled some food on his plate. "Of course people hear a dog howling when it storms," she explained patiently. "That's what dogs do when it storms."

"But I heard him!" Sean began waving his hands in the air. "I told you I heard a crying dog!"

Angel chewed slowly on a piece of lettuce, staring at her brother in fascination. There really seemed to be something clinically wrong with him.

"And that's not all!" Sean's cuff went in his sauce. "Mr. Stucker actually saw the ghost! He saw him walking along the beach in the rain with the dog. He says it was too dark to see him clearly, but they walked right into the bluff and disappeared."

Angel turned to her mother. "I think you should take away his television privileges. It's beginning to affect what there is of his mind."

"Honey," Denise said. "I think maybe your friend Mr. Stucker just likes to tell stories."

"No, it's true," Sean insisted. "I know it's true. I told you, I saw him. Billy Spatano. I saw him in my room!"

Angel couldn't help feeling sorry for Denise. She may have been pretty peculiar herself lately, but she didn't deserve a son like this.

"And that's not all," Sean prattled on. "Things move by themselves. You know, like all that stuff getting into the living room yesterday? And sometimes, instead of the dog I heard crying, people hear a motorcycle. Mr. Stucker even says he came home one time really early in the morning and he saw a riderless bike cutting across our lawn!" He slammed his hands on the table and knocked over the salt. "What do you think about that?" he crowed.

"I think your Mr. Stucker's been hitting the gin, that's what I think," Angel said.

Sean stuck his tongue out at her. "Okay, okay, so what about *this*? This one family who lived here, they used to wake up in the middle of the night and hear Elvis Presley singing."

"Ugh," said Angel. "Elvis Presley. That would scare anybody."

※　　※　　※

Like ghosts themselves, the sounds of talk and laughter drifted from the kitchen through the old house. Up they went, floating past the first floor, weaving past the second floor, and slipping, finally, into the attic. It was in the attic, sealed shut since the 1950s, that William Joseph Spatano listened to the sounds. He'd used to laugh like that. He blew a perfect smoke ring into the lightless, airless room. A long, long time ago.

William Joseph Spatano was tall and slightly stocky, and he wore his dark hair short and slicked-up at the back with a thick shock overhanging his forehead like a waterfall. He had strong, sharp features, and eyes so brown they looked almost black. His friends had called him B.J. "Hey, B.J.!" they'd used to say. "What's the good word? What's happenin', man?" B.J. had been nineteen years old the November night in 1959 when the bike he was riding crashed in a storm. And he was nineteen now. Nineteen, and with what his father would have called a bad attitude.

Tonight, lying on his old, broken bed, his dog, Sparky, beside him, B.J. was thinking about all the other nights he'd lain up here, smoking a cigarette while he stared into the past, reliving his life, moment by moment and day by day. Over and over and over again. He rarely left the attic. In three and a half decades the farthest he'd gone from this room was the shore below the bluff. B.J. placed a hand on Sparky's head. He was thinking, too, of the other voices he'd heard in this house over the endless years. Those voices had bugged him. Disturbed him. Threatened him. But he'd always known how to handle them.

He'd been alone here since his family had moved to Florida not long after his death, and alone was how he planned to stay. This place was his. This house, this room, the beach outside, the bike hidden at the back of the garage, the small black-and-brown dog whose chin rested on his leg—it was all he'd ever had, and all he wanted. He wasn't going to lose it, not any of it, by letting strangers take over his home.

A fresh wave of laughter simmered through the floor. "The Listers," he said to Sparky. He pronounced each name clearly and carefully, spitting them into the air, "Denise. Sean. Angel."

Sparky whimpered softly. B.J. closed his eyes.

Most people didn't need much prodding, but Denise, Sean, and Angel were not behaving as they should. Making noises in the night hadn't upset them. Dumping their belongings in the living room hadn't frightened them. Putting things where they shouldn't be didn't seem to distress them.

And the boy, of course—the boy was a problem. Sometimes a ghost could be seen against its will by the psychic, by the very young or old, by the very ill, or even by the very lonely. But it didn't really matter what the reason was. What mattered was that he *was* seen. Seen and possibly heard. Which meant that he had to be careful. He couldn't come out when the boy was around.

Sparky's ears went up as more shrieks echoed in the room.

"I'm not worried," B.J. assured him. "They can laugh all they want." He blew another perfect smoke ring over Sparky's head. "Because they won't be laughing long."

※　　※　　※

"Come on, Spark!" B.J. stopped in the hallway and lit a cigarette, his face caught for a second in the glow from the match, the strong features, the scar over the right eye. "Let's go out," he called. "We have some work to do."

Tail wagging, Sparky followed B.J. down the attic stairs, through the wall, and into the second-floor hallway. There was a light showing under Denise's door, but it was outside of Sean's that B.J. stopped to listen. He could just make out the sound of a small boy snoring, fast asleep.

"Coast's clear," he whispered. Sparky jumped at his knees. B.J. looked down. "Race you!" he shouted, and he ran for the stairs, the small dog bounding after him. When they reached the living room, B.J. checked Angel's room. The light was still on there as well. He gave Sparky the okay sign. "Home free," he told him. "This is gonna be a piece of cake." He slammed the front door behind them.

B.J.'s Vincent Black Shadow, which he'd gotten in 1959, was hidden at the back of the garage, under a pile of rotting, paint-splattered blankets and behind a wall of furniture left by previous tenants. The house had been neglected, the garden had been allowed to go wild, but the old bike still looked new.

Sparky started barking as B.J. wheeled the Vincent from the garage. After B.J. had died, Sparky had sat by the bike for a week, howling and crying, until B.J.'s father had taken him to the pound to be destroyed. "Good riddance to bad rubbish," the old man had said, meaning both the son and the dog.

"It's okay, boy. Shhh." B.J. leaned down and

41

scratched Sparky behind the ears. He wasn't sure that Sean could hear them, but he couldn't take the chance that the dog might wake him up. Not before he'd had a chance to scare Denise. She might be too self-absorbed to have noticed anything else he'd done so far, but she would notice a 1000 cc motorcycle roaring across the lawn by itself. "It's all right," he comforted Sparky. "Be cool." B.J. hummed an old Everly Brothers' song as he wheeled the bike to the back of the house. Denise's light was still on; she was up. He came to a stop under her window, hidden from view by a thick maple tree.

Sometimes, when the night was very dark or the air was very sweet, sometimes he liked to come out here and start her up. Once in awhile he might ride her around the yard a few times, just to feel what it was like again, but usually he just sat here, going nowhere, listening to the engine, almost able to remember how it felt to be alive, to ride into the wind, hunched over the bars, the road like a tunnel leading straight to your dreams. But he never went onto the road. Not even after all these years. And he never let the house out of his sight, either, as if he were afraid it might just disappear while he was gone. Then he wouldn't only be trapped in time: he'd be trapped in time and lost in space, with no direction home at all.

B.J. straddled the bike, his eyes on the black, enormous sky. Tonight, though, was different. Tonight was not for remembering. Tonight was for getting back his own.

Angel reached into the aluminum box and pulled out the mail. "Oh, thank you, God!" she cried, recognizing Gavin's small, neat handwriting on the back of a postcard of the painting *Irises,* and Lindy's unmistakable scrawl, silver ink on a scarlet envelope. She gave the letters an ecstatic kiss. She was so lonely and missed her friends so much that hearing from them had become the most important thing in her life. Even more important than the Saturday-night phone calls with her father. She wrote to Lindy almost every day, and every night, after writing to Gavin, she fell asleep with her Walkman on, listening to his favorite tapes, imagining she was being held in his arms.

Still standing by the mailbox at the side of the road, Angel read the card from Gavin. Like all of his correspondence, it was no more than a note telling her what he'd done the night before, how everybody said hello, and that he missed her. As a pen pal, Gavin, well, he was a good football player, but Angel didn't care. What was important was that he always wrote "I love you" at the bottom. She smiled to herself as she finished reading this week's installment and tucked the card into her pocket. Not only had he written "I love you," but he'd filled the bottom of the card with kisses.

Angel started back to the house, tearing open the dark red envelope as she walked slowly across the grass. Lindy's letters were something else. Long and rambling, they were packed with gossip and stories and details of life in Lisson Park. They almost made Angel forget, if only for just a few minutes, that she was hundreds of miles away. Laughing over the story of Lindy's last driving lesson, Angel climbed the steps to the porch. She reached out and put her hand on the doorknob. She pulled. Nothing happened. She pulled again. The door seemed to be locked— but it couldn't be locked, because she'd just come out of it. She gave the door a kick. *Nothing works right in this stupid house,* she fumed. *You turned on a light and the light went off. You turned off a light and the light went on. You opened a door and it locked behind you.* Giving the door a farewell kick, she marched back down the steps and around to the back of the house. "I wish the whole place would just fall down," she muttered to herself as she angrily marched into the kitchen.

One minute, Angel was walking toward the table. The next thing she knew, bells were ringing and she was flat on her face on the black-and-white tiles.

"Sean Lister!" Angel bellowed. "Sean Lister, you moron, I am going to kill you! I mean it this time. I am going to cut you up into tiny pieces and feed you to the seagulls."

At that moment Denise appeared in the doorway, buttoning her blouse and talking to herself as she came into the room. "It's the strangest thing," she was saying, "but I thought I smelled cigarette smoke upstairs again."

Angel got to her feet. "Mom," she said, brushing off her favorite pink slacks. "Mom, you have got to do something about your son."

Denise didn't even glance at her. She went straight to the stove and turned on the jet under the teapot. "And yesterday there was the strongest odor of motor oil in the bathroom."

Angel picked up the piece of string that had tripped her and held it in the air. The bells that had

44

been tied to it jingled. "Mom, will you just look at what Weirdo Boy's done now? He could have killed me."

Finally, Denise looked over. "Don't tell me," she begged. "It's another of his ghost traps."

"*And* he locked me out of the house when I went to get the mail." Angel threw herself into the nearest chair. It was pathetic, really. Sean had never been what she would call normal, but his ghost obsession was getting out of hand. Now he was trying to catch the ghost. But did her mother do anything about it? No, her mother did *not* do anything about it. Not even when Denise herself had nearly been drowned in Sean's flour-bomb trap. "I mean, really, Mom, you can't let him go on like this. I caught him sneaking out in his pajamas last night to see if he could hear that motorcycle again."

Denise dumped two heaping spoonfuls of instant coffee into a cup and sighed. "I'm sure it's just a passing phase. Because of the move and everything."

Angel felt like banging her head on the table. "*A passing phase?* Mom, he's hallucinating. Your son heard a ghost riding a motorcycle around the yard when you and I didn't hear anything."

"To tell you the truth," said Denise, "I'm so exhausted by the end of the day that half the time I fall asleep at my desk with the lights still on."

"You're making excuses for him again," Angel snapped. She was as tired of hearing her mother's excuses for Sean as she was of hearing how tired her mother was all the time. "But what do you think the neighbors are going to say if they see him running around the lawn in his pajamas, looking for a ghost on a Harley Davidson? Even in Midville, that's pretty strange."

Denise held up her hands. "Please. I can't think about it this minute. I'll try to talk to him before I leave, but not until after I've had my coffee." She poured boiling water into her cup. "If it's not one thing, it's another," she mumbled half to herself. "Now the whole diner has to be repainted. I told them I wanted cornflower blue, but for some reason they painted it turquoise. The place looks like a pizzeria."

Angel stopped listening. All her mother seemed to do these days was worry about the diner. There was never anything to eat in the house, the laundry basket was overflowing, and the new curtains she'd been promised had been put off for a new pair of glasses for Android Child. She started reading Lindy's letter again. Lindy was dreading going back to school because it meant the end of spending all day on the beach and partying all night. Angel made a face. Her own life was so boring and lonely that she was almost looking forward to starting school. At least it would be something to do besides chores. And even though Midville High was bound to be filled with cretins, it had suddenly occurred to her that there had to be a group she could relate to as well. They couldn't all be from the lost planet, could they? There had to be some trendsetting, popular kids who would welcome someone like her with open arms.

"Angel!"

She looked up. Her mother was yelling again.

"Angel, are you in some sort of trance or something? What are your shoes doing in the refrigerator?" Denise was standing in front of the opened fridge, holding Angel's sneakers by their laces. They were stuffed with carrots.

"I didn't do that. What would I do a stupid thing like that for?"

"And what's this?" She removed a bundle of clothes from the vegetable crisper.

"Dirty laundry?"

Denise didn't think that was funny. "Is this your idea of a joke?" She shook the clothes in Angel's direction.

"Me?" Angel's voice was shrill with indignation. "Why do you always blame *me* for everything around here?"

Denise glared at her. "Don't I have enough to worry about?" She threw the clothes from the crisper onto the counter. "I want some help and cooperation around her for a change."

"For a change?" Angel couldn't believe her ears. She'd done nothing but work, work, work since they'd arrived. What was her mother trying to do to her?

"Especially from you, young lady." Denise folded her arms across her chest. "Once the diner opens, I'm going to have to give it all my time for awhile, you know. I hope you understand that I'm depending on you to look after your brother and the house."

"Me?" Angel squeaked.

Denise picked up her bag from the counter. "Yes, you. You're sixteen. It's about time you started doing some of the cooking and cleaning around here." She picked up a pillowcase and threw it at Angel. "And washing."

"But, Mom . . ."

"I expect this house to be spotless when I get back," she shouted as she stalked from the room. "And supper to be on the table!" The front door slammed.

Angel stared after her. She knew what her mother was trying to do to her. She was trying to turn her into Cinderella. Tears filled her eyes. It was just as well she didn't have any social life. She wouldn't be able to enjoy it anyway.

William Joseph Spatano was sitting on his bed, looking out the window at Sean fooling around with his bicycle in the yard, and feeling a little discouraged.

"It beats me," B.J. said to Sparky. "Usually all I hafta do is play 'Hound Dog' and they're back in their cars and on their way to a motel."

But not the Listers. He could produce the hound dog, Elvis, and the entire staff of Sun Records, and all that would happen was Sean would get so excited he'd break his glasses again and Denise and Angel would argue with each other about whose fault all the noise was.

B.J. watched Sean struggling to put the chain back on. He smiled, reminded of his own kid brother. The way the kid was doing it, he'd be there till he was thirty. Still, the boy was getting to be more and more of a problem. He'd made so much noise on the Vincent the other night, he was sure Denise was going to come to the window, see the unmanned bike tearing across the lawn, and scream. But all that had happened was that Sean had come racing out of the house, barefoot and wearing pajamas, calling, "Billy! Billy! Wait for me!" The smile vanished. *Billy*. No one had ever called him Billy except his mother. B.J. had had to ride out onto the road to get away from the kid. He'd had to park in a clump of trees three blocks away, waiting till he was sure Sean had given up and gone back to bed. And now, of course, Sean was hot on his trail, laying traps and skulking around the yard, looking for B.J. long after Denise thought he was tucked up in bed.

But even more discouraging was the fact that his problem with Denise and Angel was the opposite of his problem with Sean. No matter what he did, they acted as though he didn't exist. He turned off lights, and they turned them back on. He opened doors, and they closed them. He left faucets running, and Denise yelled at the kids. He moved things around, Denise blamed Angel—and Angel blamed Sean. He played music in the early hours of the morning, and they didn't hear it. He locked Angel out, and she got mad at the house.

He could hear Denise's car pull out of the driveway. "We're just gonna hafta figure out what makes them tick," said B.J. thoughtfully.

Discouraged, but not defeated.

After all, most people didn't care for ghosts. It was just a question of finding their weakness; of locating the point where they had to give in. He blew a perfect smoke ring over Sparky's head.

There wasn't much to learn about Denise by checking out her room. She read cookbooks and books on managing your own small business. She owned clothes, a hair dryer, and an alarm clock. She had an awful lot of bills, paint charts, and handwritten menus piled up on her desk. But that, as far as B.J. could tell, was about it. *Some life,* he thought as he put a manual on menu planning back in its place. *It wasn't much better than being a ghost in an attic.*

Angel's room, however, was crammed with things. While Angel herself, grumbling and thumping around, cleaned the house and grappled with the old washing machine in the basement, B.J. whiled away the afternoon by going through her possessions.

He looked through her closet, her dresser, and her jewelry box. Angel had a preference for pink that he didn't share. He flipped through her photo albums and scrapbooks. There were a lot of pictures of Angel with other kids. She was always at the center of the groups, always smiling. It was hard to believe it was the same girl. There were dozens and dozens of clippings about rock-and-roll bands B.J. had never heard of. A lot of the musicians—if they were musicians—looked like girls. *Elvis will always be king,* thought B.J. *There ain't no competition.* He read Angel's diary, full of details of the things that she did—the parties and games and shopping expeditions and what she wore to them and who was there—and, more recently, complaints. It was boring. Angel never wore the same thing twice, but the things she did were always with the same people, doing and saying the same things. He read the letter she was writing to Lindy, full of more complaints about Denise and Sean and the house. It was boring. He read the letters she'd received from her friends in Lisson Park since she'd been here. These were the most boring of all. Lindy's went on for pages and pages. *How can anyone talk so much about shopping?* B.J. wondered. Her description of a shoe sale almost put him to sleep. And as for this jerk, Gavin, the one whose picture Angel kept under her pillow, his idea of a letter was three lines about himself on the back of a postcard with a buncha dumb flowers on it.

B.J. stretched out on Angel's bed, going through the box that held her most special things. Small things, mostly. A faded strip of photo-booth snapshots of her and a slightly horsey-looking girl he assumed must be Lindy. A box containing a lock of hair. A necklace made of painted macaroni. He became so absorbed in an old photograph of Angel and Denise riding a Ferris wheel, their arms around each other, "Me and Mom" written on the back in a childish scrawl, that he didn't hear Angel come into the room.

"Sean?"

He looked up to see her standing in the doorway, a puzzled expression on her face.

"Sean?" she repeated. "Are you in here?"

B.J. tossed a purple ticket stub back onto the bed. "What I want to know is, what anyone would save that for," he commented. "I mean, it's not like you can use it again or even remember what the flick was."

"Sean?" Angel's eyes traveled around the room. "I know you're in here. I can feel—" She was staring at the box B.J. was going through. And at the pile of things beside it.

"My letters! My diary!" Her voice broke with fury. "Sean Lister," she screamed, "this time you die!"

B.J. leaned back, putting his arms under his head. "Give the kid a break," he said. "Even if he *had* done it, reading your letters would be enough punishment for anybody."

51

"Where are you?" she demanded. Angel yanked open the closet. She looked under the bed.

B.J. smiled. "He's not here," he said. "Unless he's invisible."

Angel turned on her heel and charged from the room, still screaming. "You listen to me, you little iguana with glasses," she raged. "If you so much as breathe near my stuff again, I'll take your stupid telescope and throw it over the cliff."

B.J. followed. She rushed through the living room, thundered up the stairs, pounded back down the stairs, and only came to a stop when she reached the kitchen. There was no sign of her brother anywhere. "I was sure he was in my room," she mumbled. "Where could he be hiding?"

B.J. slid onto the counter. "I wouldn't worry about Sean," he said. "Your mother's going to be pretty mad if she gets home and there's nothing to eat."

Almost as though she had actually heard him, Angel glanced at the clock. "I don't believe this!" she wailed. "Look at the time, and I haven't even started supper yet!"

"Shake a leg, sweetheart." There was something about seeing Angel in a panic that almost put him in a good mood. "Time to rattle those pots and pans." A very good mood.

Angel wrenched open the refrigerator door and stared in. "Chopped meat," she announced. "What am I supposed to do with chopped meat?"

B.J. peered over her shoulders. "Hamburgers," he suggested. "Spaghetti and meatballs. I always liked spaghetti and meatballs."

"Meatloaf," Angel said, ripping the meat package off the shelf. "Meatloaf can't be hard to make."

B.J. watched in disbelief as Angel took the lump of meat and savagely squashed it into a loaf pan. "Maybe you should check it out in one of your mother's cookbooks," he suggested. "Even I know you're supposed to put somethin' in it. Eggs or somethin'."

But Angel had no time for cookbooks or eggs. She turned on the oven, flung the pan in, and slammed the door. "Potatoes!" she cried. "I wonder how you boil potatoes."

B.J. whistled. "Brother, you are going to make some poor Joe a real lousy wife one day."

"Potatoes are too much trouble," Angel decided. "I think I'll just open a can of corn."

At the sound of Denise's car pulling into the driveway, B.J. jumped down from the counter and shambled toward the cellar door. As he passed the table, he gathered up the plates and cutlery Angel had put out and left them on the floor. From outside he could hear the frantic sound of a bicycle bell, and then Sean's voice saying, "Mom, look! Look, Mom! Billy fixed my bike? Now I can ride to school like all the other kids!" B.J. hadn't intended to repair the bike, but Sean had gone to his room crying because he couldn't get the chain on, and there it was, lying in the driveway. Standing there, looking down at it, B.J. had thought for a moment that it was his brother Danny's bike, lying on its side the way Danny'd always left it. The next thing he knew, the bike was fixed. *It doesn't count*, he'd told himself. *It's just a bike. He'll take it with him when they go.*

B.J. took the cellar stairs two at a time. He

removed the clean laundry from the dryer, put it back in the washer, and turned it on. That done, he returned to the kitchen. Angel was staring into the saucepan of corn as though she expected it to speak. B.J. wafted through the back door just as Denise and Sean entered from the front.

"Sean, please . . ." Denise was saying.

"No, really, Mom. It had to be Billy. Who else could've fixed my bike?"

"Sean! I've just about had it with this ghost of yours, do you hear me? I don't want to—" She broke off in mid-sentence. And then she started speaking again, horror in her voice. "Angel! Angel, what's going on here? What are the dishes doing on the floor? Why isn't supper ready? Is *that* supper? We're having a can of corn for supper?"

Smiling to himself, B.J. glided across the yard, singing another old song to himself. "Yakety yak," he sang. "Don't talk back."

Chapter 4
All Shook Up

A group of chattering girls swept past Angel. One of them, a tall, thin blonde who, for some reason, reminded her a little of Lindy, whacked Angel with her shoulder bag. The girl didn't even look around to say she was sorry, but tossed her hair over her shoulder with a shrill giggle. The door to the Midville High cafeteria shut behind them. The din of talk and laughter drifted out. *I feel like a ghost,* thought Angel. *That's what I feel like, a ghost.*

Angel was standing at the entrance, steeling herself to go in and sit alone at a corner table, writing another letter to Lindy. A ghost: that was exactly what she was. She was here, with all these people, but as far as they were concerned, she didn't exist. They looked right through her. If they didn't look right through her, they stared at her as though she had her clothes on backward, or two heads. "Look at that girl's nails," someone in her gym class had whispered loudly yesterday. And she, Angel Lister, a trendsetter of The Park, one of the East Coast's most prestigious private schools, had gone home and taken off all ten shades of pink polish, diluting the remover with her tears.

She cried herself to sleep every night. Ever since school had started, as soon as she turned out the lights, turned on her Walkman, and curled up in bed, the tears had begun to flow. Angel had really convinced herself that all she had to do was turn up at Midville High and everyone would be fighting one another to make her part of their group. But they weren't. All of a sudden she was the outsider, the girl who didn't fit in. The kids here dressed differently and talked differently than the kids in Lisson Park. They had different rules. She wore her best skirt and blouse the first day of school, only to discover that everyone who counted was wearing jeans. The first time she answered a question in history class, everyone laughed at the way she said *Washington*. At her old school there was always a mixer for each class at the beginning of the term, but not here. Here, everyone carried book bags, and no one was into pastels or loafers. Angel's French teacher couldn't understand her accent. Her math teacher couldn't understand her division. The boys were loud and dorky. The girls were cliquey and styleless. And the cheerleaders had turned her down flat.

Joking and jostling each other, several pimply boys pushed past her. Angel raised her chin. It was go in now, or starve. And she couldn't afford to starve at the moment. She needed her strength for her misery. Taking a deep breath, she followed them in.

Angel crossed to the line. As part of Denise's anti-life policy, which provided no money for any essential "extras," such as new clothes, Angel had been bringing her lunch from home the past few days. But she'd been so busy getting Sean's breakfast and making him a sandwich this morning, she hadn't had time to fix anything for herself. She gazed at the menu, looking for something that was cheap but plentiful. Not only did misery require that she keep up her strength, it seemed to require large amounts of food as well.

"I mean, my god," a vaguely familiar voice beside her was saying, "did you see what she was wearing today? She can't possibly buy her clothes around here."

Angel froze.

There was a high-pitched cackle. Then another voice, also faintly familiar, said, "Those shoes! Did you see those shoes? I can't believe she has the nerve to go out in public like that. I wouldn't wear them on a bet!"

Her face still pointed toward the menu, her body rigid, Angel looked over out of the corners of her eyes. No wonder the voices sounded familiar. They belonged to Silvia Samson and May Lewis, who sat across the room from her in history. Silvia Samson and May Lewis were captain and cocaptain of the cheerleaders, and two of the most popular girls in the entire school. They were the girls Angel *should* be friends with.

"I almost feel sorry for her," said the first voice, which belonged to Silvia. "I mean, she could almost be pretty if she knew anything about makeup."

Angel could feel the blood rushing to her face. *Her.* They were talking about her. Her clothes. Her shoes. Her makeup.

May snorted. "With that hair? Are you kidding? It looks like it was cut with a nail clipper."

Not *her* hair. Angel's hair was long and curly, and up until a few weeks ago it had been cut by Jeremy at

57

Lisson Park's most exclusive salon. Angel started to breathe again. They weren't talking about her, after all. She turned to look at them.

At almost the same moment, Silvia turned, too.

Angel's heart began to pound. This was the opportunity she'd been waiting for. She'd been trying to catch their attention all week long, but somehow they'd never seemed to notice her. Angel smiled right into Silvia's face.

Silvia looked through her. "There she is," she breathed. "You know, I think she's put another hole in her ears. She'll have one in her nose next."

Suze Adams, thought Angel. *It has to be.* Suze Adams was the smartest person in Angel's history class, and the weirdest. Her hair was cut as short as a boy's, and she wore three earrings in each ear. She seemed to dress only in black. Yesterday, as Angel had been walking to class, Suze had come up to her and started talking about the French Revolution. "What do you think, personally, about guillotining?" she'd asked. Angel hadn't known what to say.

May looked around.

Angel's smile got brighter. She cleared her throat to speak. *Oh, boy, Suze Adams,* she was going to say. *Isn't she just the pits?*

May gazed through her, too. "Sometimes I don't think there's one interesting person in this school besides us," said May.

Sitting at her corner of the corner table, Angel ate her lunch and wrote her letter.

It's not bad enough that Sean's gone completely nuts since we got here, but now my

58

mother's getting worse, too. She's traded the BMW for a secondhand van. Metallic blue! Can you believe it? I think maybe she's trying to recapture her lost youth or something. I sure wish I could recapture *my* lost youth. What a wasteland! You just wouldn't believe how they dress and act up here. Really. Talk about the living dead. I'm practically the only human in a high school full of zombies. No wonder they stare at me all the time. They've hardly ever seen a real person before.

A loud cackle of laughter rose above the general hubbub. Angel looked over to the crowded table in the center of the room.

Actually, there are two girls in my history class who aren't zombies. They're the only interesting people in this dump besides me, and we're getting pretty friendly. We had lunch together today. Their names are Silvia Samoon and May Lewis. They're cheerleaders, of course.

❋ ❋ ❋

He should never have fixed the bike. It was all Sean had needed to convince himself that the ghost wanted to be friends with him. Now he'd stopped trying to catch B.J. and was leaving him notes instead.

Dear Billy: I know Mr. Stucker says you shot someone, but I don't care.

Dear Billy: I know you're not all bad. You can't be. The bike works great.

Dear Billy: You know you can trust me. I want to be your friend.

Now B.J. could only risk coming out of the attic when he was sure Sean was at school. B.J. turned the page with a sigh. Like his old man always said, "If you're nice to people, they take advantage." Only his old man, of course, had had *him* in mind when he said it. His old man had meant that he'd given him a home and fed him and clothed him, and look at what he'd got in return. "What'd I do to deserve a bum like you?" his old man had meant.

It was Friday afternoon, and B.J. was stretched out on the living room sofa, a couple of throw pillows under his head, going through a pile of Angel's magazines. No way he'd admit it, but he was almost enjoying himself. For over thirty years the outside world had stopped existing for him, and now here it was, staring him in the face. Cellulite. Cholesterol. Pollution. Food additives. Aerobics. Crash helmets. The ozone layer. Tummy tucks. Killer cigarettes.

It just went to show you, you couldn't turn your back for a minute. He'd never heard of half these things. He started reading an article on safe sex. He could hardly believe it. When he'd been sixteen, you couldn't even whisper the word *sex,* never mind write about it in a magazine.

He turned the page, his eyes on a photograph of two beautiful girls modeling cycling shorts and Lycra tops. "Flexible Fun" said the caption. B.J. whistled.

The other thing he couldn't get over was the clothes. What had happened to long, full skirts with poodles on them, and bobby socks? What had happened to white cotton bras and cardigans? Maybe it wasn't that he'd died too young, maybe the trouble was that he'd been born too soon.

He tossed the magazine aside and picked up another. A piece of rose-colored paper fell out. *If it's pink, it's gotta be Angel's,* B.J. thought. He picked it up. Another letter to Lindy. He couldn't get over how they never ran out of things to say to each other. Even though he knew how boring Angel's letters were, he couldn't stop himself from beginning to read. More complaints about Sean and her room. More moans about how she had to do everything around the house. A long paragraph about her new friends, Silvia and May.

B.J. frowned. Who the heck were Silvia and May? Silvia, apparently, was the prettiest, most sophisticated girl in Midville, and May was the funniest and drove a lilac sports car.

> Last night, Silvia had a little get-together so I could meet her closest friends, and it was really neat. You should see Silvia's house! It makes Gavin's look like a bungalow. I didn't even think they had houses like that in Midville.

B.J. checked the date on the letter. "Last night" would have been Wednesday. Wednesday night, Angel had stayed home, like she did every night. He always heard her when he and Sparky went on their nocturnal rounds, trying to find something short of attacking Denise that would finally catch her attention.

The sound of angry voices in the driveway yanked him out of his thoughts. A car door slammed.

"Sean Lister!" Denise was screaming. "What is all over the living room windows? Is that soap?"

A second door slammed closed. "Me?" Sean screeched. "Mom, I didn't do that. Billy—"

"Sean, please. I don't know what's got into you

61

lately, but I can't take much more. I never know what I'm going to wake up to. Garbage dumped on the lawn, mud all over the kitchen, paint in the bathtub—"

"But it's Billy. Mr. Stucker says it's because he came to a bad end. That's why he can't rest. Mr. Stucker says—"

"Sean!"

Angel's voice joined in as the third car door shut. "He's sick, Mom, I've been trying to tell you that for ages. The boy needs help."

B.J. looked over at the clock on the mantel. Seven o'clock! What had happened to the afternoon?

"But it's *Billy*—"

"No more!" Denise ordered.

B.J. jumped. For Pete's sake, they were nearly at the house. He jammed the letter back in the magazine and sprinted up the stairs.

The front door opened. "What's all this now?" Denise let out a low moan. "I don't believe you, Angel. You've left your junk all over the couch!"

Angel responded with her usual righteous indignation. "No, I didn't. It's Sean! Sean's been in my room again! Messing around with my things."

"No, I didn't! I wasn't even here. I was with you guys!"

"Don't look at me. *I* didn't do it."

"And neither did I."

"Then who did?"

"Stop it! Both of you!" Denise sounded as if she were about to explode. "I've just about had all I can stand of your endless bickering."

"But I'm telling you, I didn't do it. . . ." Sean

protested. "How could I do it when I wasn't even here?"

"Well, someone was," said Angel.

There was something in her tone that made B.J. stop in his tracks. He frowned. It bothered him, that tone. It was like she was thinking.

Denise heard it, too. "Don't *you* start," she snapped. "I've got enough with your brother."

"But, Mom, Sean's right. He wasn't here. He—"

"I mean it," Denise said. "I don't want to hear one more word about this ghost."

Maybe just one more word, B.J. thought as he melted through the wall to the attic stairs.

It was so simple, he couldn't understand why he hadn't thought of it before. Denise. She was older; she was a mother. She had to be the Lister most susceptible to terror. All he had to do was drive her to work one morning. That was all, just lean over and take the wheel. "Excuse me, Mrs. Lister, but I'll drive now." All he had to do was put his foot on the gas. He'd show her how to take that sharp curve on Skidmoor on only two wheels. He'd teach her how to thread the needle all the way from Dogwood into town. He'd get that old van of hers moving like it had never moved before. "You drive like the devil," his old man had always told him. "Like the devil himself." Well, maybe he'd prove his old man right, again. If anyone could turn the drive through Midville's quiet, tree-lined roads into a ride through hell, William Joseph Spatano was that person. He was an expert on rides through hell.

Of course, to carry out his plan, he would have to

63

leave the house. And the street. And the neighbor-hood. Not things he was delighted about doing, having managed to avoid them for so long. On the other hand, the Listers had upset his life so much, it was worth a little extra trouble to see them go. *Don't sweat it,* he reassured himself. *It's not like you'll be on the bike.* He couldn't do that: he couldn't take the bike out. But the van was different. The van held no bad memories. Denise would get them back again. The house wouldn't disappear. And, anyway, it might not be so bad, going into town. He might see some chicks in those cycling shorts.

The engine of the van kicked over, and B.J. woke with a start. Of course, the other thing he had to do to carry out his plan was to get up before noon. He blinked in the thin morning light. "Geez," he mumbled, throwing himself from the bed, "it's practically dawn."

Not even bothering to worry about Sean for a change, he raced down the stairs. *You jerk,* he told himself. *You've really blown it this time. How're ya gonna scare her if you can't even get up?* He hurled himself through the door and was halfway across the lawn before he realized that the van was still in the driveway. He slowed down. Denise was sitting behind the wheel, staring out at the house, almost as though she'd been waiting for him.

It's an omen, he thought. *It's gonna be all right.* Feeling pretty pleased with himself, B.J. hopped into the passenger seat. "Okay, I'm here." He snapped his fingers. "You can go now."

Denise sighed and turned the key in the ignition.

She started pumping the gas pedal. The van bleated hoarsely. She wasn't going anywhere, that was for sure. Denise started to cry.

"Turn it off," B.J. ordered. He really hated crying. What was the good of tears? They didn't change anything. They didn't get you anywhere. He faced the passenger window so he wouldn't see them. "Turn it off before you kill the battery." People cried to make you feel sorry for them. But he'd vowed a long time ago not to feel sorry for anyone ever again. Not to feel sorry, and not to try to help.

Denise turned the van off. She leaned her head on the steering wheel, sobbing in earnest. "Why are you doing this to me?" she asked in a choked voice. "Why won't you go?"

Was she talking to him? He glanced over. No, she was not talking to him. She was pounding the dashboard, tears streaming down her face. He couldn't remember the last time he'd seen anyone cry like this. Angel didn't count. Angel went hysterical every time she found a split end. He stared at the hedge along the side of the drive. "I could've used you at my funeral," said B.J. "Every eye was dry."

Denise fumbled in her pocket for a tissue. "Why doesn't anything ever go right for me?" she demanded.

"You?" She made him want to laugh. "Why doesn't anything go right for *you?* What about me? I'm dead, and I can't even get any peace and quiet."

"I don't believe this." Her voice broke. "I just don't believe my life is turning out like this. I'm trying so hard. . . ."

B.J. shifted uncomfortably in his seat. She sounded tired—tired and scared. More scared, maybe, than someone threading the needle all the way from Dogwood into town. Reluctantly, and against his better judgment, he turned and looked at her. It was the first time he'd really looked at her since she'd invaded his home. She *looked* tired and scared, too. The hand that was wiping the tears away was thin and pale. He'd been seeing her as strong and determined, his foe. As Mrs. Lister, the woman who took over. Who had just moved in and took over everything, bossed you around, pushed you out of your own home—just like Renee, his stepmother, had done. But all of a sudden, she didn't seem like his enemy. She was just a mother with two kids and no husband and no understanding whatsoever of the workings of the internal combustion engine— a mother who was having a hard time. The idea of terrifying her was beginning to lose its appeal.

B.J. vaulted out of the seat. "It's probably no big deal," he said. "I'll take a look at the engine."

Denise started talking to herself again. "It serves me right," she said. "I should never have bought this ridiculous van. I only did it because I knew Marshall would hate it." She blew her nose.

B.J. smiled at the distributor cap. He'd used to do things just because he knew they'd rile his old man.

Denise's tears snuffled to an end. "Okay, that's enough." She took a deep breath. "You're not the only person with problems, Denise Lister," she said. "Sitting here feeling sorry for yourself isn't going to get you anywhere. If you have to walk to town, then you'll walk."

"That should do it," B.J. called over his shoulder. "Turn 'er over."

"One more try," said Denise, her hand on the key, "and then I walk."

The engine sputtered for a second, then caught.

Denise laughed with relief. "Thank you!" she cried, kissing the steering wheel. "Thank you!"

"Don't mention it," said William Joseph Spatano, heading toward the house. As he reached the path, he began to hum a song about Memphis, Tennessee.

The sun slid slowly across the sky as B.J. wandered through the house, from one room to another, restless as a breeze.

He wasn't sure why, but ever since getting the van started that morning, he'd been thinking about his mother. Not Renee, his father's wife, but his real mother. He couldn't remember anything about her, not one tiny thing. What he remembered was what he'd imagined about her—her smell, her voice, the way she'd held him in her arms. Once he was old enough to understand that Renee was Danny's mother but not his—and that she didn't like him—he'd lain in bed at night making up stories about his real mother. He invented places for them to go and things for them to do together. They went to the movies and the firemen's fun-fair. They went on picnics and spent afternoons at the roller rink. They went to the lake and sailed a navy of small plastic boats, and afterward they went for chocolate ice-cream cones with chocolate sprinkles. He made her up, and he made her love him. She always bought him a candy bar when she took him shopping, and her favorite color was yellow. She wore Evening in Paris, shoes with ankle straps, and lipstick the same red as a fire truck. She hated broccoli and Frank Sinatra, canasta and Broadway shows—the things that

Renee liked. She baked devil's food cake for his birthday, and she let him carve the pumpkin at Halloween. She always tucked him in at night. Dumb things like that. Kid's stuff. The only thing he didn't make up was that she'd called him Billy. That was the one thing he knew. That was written in faded blue ink on the back of the only photograph he had of her, "Mom and Billy, 1940." He'd been two when she died. Two. It was like he'd died himself.

B.J. sat at Denise's desk in the pale light of the afternoon, thinking about her sitting in the stalled van, talking to no one and crying like the last person in the world. It wasn't like he wanted her to go because he hated her. It wasn't personal. His eyes moved along the row of pictures lined up on the desk: Denise and Sean; Denise and Angel; Denise, Sean, and Angel all laughing in the snow. "I like you," he said to the Denise in the wool scarf and knit hat. "I really do. You understand that, right? It ain't personal." Denise was always trying to make things okay. She came home at night with surprises for the kids—a leftover wedge of pie, a set of glow-in-the-dark stars for Sean's ceiling, a pink ballpoint pen for the princess. "It's just, you know, it's just that I'm used to things, that's all. I was okay the way I was." Locked away. Trapped in the present, but stuck in the past. He wiped some dust from the photo with his finger. He really did like Denise. He liked to hear her singing to herself in the morning as she was getting ready for work. He liked the way she laughed. He liked that she only cried when she thought no one could hear her.

The ringing of a bicycle bell made him look out the window. Sean was coasting into the driveway, home from school. B.J. put the picture back in place. *Maybe the Listers don't really need to move out, after all,* B.J. thought as he drifted out of the room. Not absolutely. It would be a drag for them to move. It would cost a lot. Denise couldn't afford another expense. And, anyway, where would they go? Denise had enough problems without having to look for another place to live. *Come on,* he told himself, *it's not like they're gonna remodel the house or anything, is it? She can't afford to buy the kid a new bike, she ain't gonna redo the kitchen.* Besides, as soon as the diner took off, they'd take off, too. Move someplace with one of those micro-whatever-it-wases and a private bathroom for her majesty.

He stopped at the front bedroom window. Sean was spreading newspapers in the driveway. Angel was striding across the lawn toward him. For some reason, she never came home from school in a good mood.

Maybe all he and the Listers needed was a little compromise here and there. Maybe that was all. A little give-and-take. The house was big enough for all of them, really. As long as they left him alone. That was all. As long as they let him be.

"Sean!" Angel's voice was as loud and clear as gunshots in the peaceful afternoon. "Sean! Don't think you're going to sit around doing nothing all afternoon. You're going to help me do the chores."

"But, Angel, I was going to paint my bike. All the kids—"

"Don't 'but, Angel' me. You help me, you little turd, or I'll exorcise your ghost once and for all."

B.J. frowned. He wasn't sure Angel Lister knew what compromise was.

❀ ❀ ❀

Surely there's no way things can get worse than this, thought Angel as she scooped up another armful of leaves and dropped them into the bag. Wasn't it supposed to get really dark before the dawn, or something like that? Well, her life couldn't get much darker than it was now. Her mother was hardly ever around. Her father was suddenly too busy even to talk about having Angel visit him. Her teachers hated her. She had no friends. She had no fun. All she had was work, work, work. Angel, do this. Angel, do that. Angel, don't tell me you haven't finished yet. Talk about Cinderella. At least Cinderella got to go to a dance. Angel would be lucky if she ever danced again. And Cinderella wound up with a prince. The only prince in Midville was a dog. Probably a Doberman with a bad attitude. Angel sighed. Even Lindy's letters weren't cheering her up anymore. Instead, they made her feel worse. Lindy was still doing all the things they used to do together, and still having a great time, while Angel was slowly dying of loneliness. Things were so dark that she started making up a life to tell Lindy about. Telling Lindy the truth would only depress Angel more.

Angel sighed again as she glumly dragged the leaf bag across the grass. "If Lindy and Gavin could see me now, they'd just die," she grumbled, the rake bumping along behind her. "Angel Lister, casual laborer." She stared at the lawn with a sense of hopelessness. Why bother? What on earth was the point? As quickly as she raked up the leaves, new ones fell to take their place. It was exactly the same with housework. Whatever you cleaned only got dirty again.

Only in *their* house, of course, it was even worse than that, because Weirdo Boy was trying so hard to prove that there really was a ghost. You put the dirty clothes in the washing machine, and when you came back, they were still dirty—but in the dryer. You stuck a chicken in the oven, and when you came back, the oven was off and the chicken was in the sink. Things went missing—keys, books, clothes, the remote control for the TV. And things turned up—a wheelbarrow in the kitchen, someone's garbage can in the back of the van, every newspaper that should have been delivered to the other houses on Bluff Drive in a pile on their porch. Even Denise was beginning to show concern. Angel had heard her on the telephone with Marshall the other night, after Angel had gone to her room, telling him about Sean and his ghost stories. "I'm really worried," Denise had whispered. "I wonder if we should, you know, send him to someone." *Send* me *to someone,* Angel had said to herself. *Someone in Lisson Park.*

Angel leaned on her rake, gazing into space. A slight shiver ran through her. Darn Sean and his stupid ghost. Not only was he getting to Denise with his ridiculous behavior, but he was beginning to get to Angel, as well. There'd been times lately when she'd walked into an empty room and had the strange feeling that there really *was* someone there. And she was starting to hear things. Not in the middle of the night, but during the day and in the evening. And not motorcycles or whimpering dogs or Elvis Presley, but footsteps and laughter and even snatches of talk, as though someone were whispering from across a noisy room. There'd been times lately, when she'd almost thought Sean was telling the truth.

With a heavy sigh, Angel brought her eyes back to earth. She was staring down at the brown, patchy lawn and the scattered leaves, but she was seeing something else: an image. It was the image of a window: a small window, high in the roof. Slowly, Angel looked up again. She hadn't been gazing into space at all: she'd been gazing at the roof of the house. A conversation that seemed to have taken place a lifetime ago came back to her. Sean saying that there was definitely an attic. Her mother saying that if there was, it would only be big enough to store screens in. Angel stared at the window. As small as it was, she could imagine it hung with curtains. She could see her face in it, looking longingly across the water. Maybe, just maybe, her mother had been wrong again. . . .

B.J. was sprawled across his bed, flipping through the pages of a thirty-something-year-old motorcycle magazine. It was a magazine he had read before, and it wasn't half as interesting as one of Angel's. He let it drop and looked out the window. The turning leaves made him think of apple cider and long rides in the country. Made him think, for some reason, of laughter and rain. There was no sign of Angel. Her rake and her leaf bag were under the half-dead oak. *She's probably taking a break to freshen her lipstick,* B.J. decided. *She's probably in the bathroom crying because she broke another nail.* He shook his head. She was supposed to be working, but instead she'd been banging in and out of the house all morning. Several times he'd seen her marching around the yard or staring up at the house with this look on her face. He rubbed clean a circle on the glass. He wasn't sure he liked the look. He'd been seeing it a lot lately. She'd come into a room, she'd cock her head, and she'd get that exact same look on her face. Like something wasn't right. Like she was trying to figure something out.

There was a sharp whine beside him.

B.J. looked over. Sparky's ears were raised, and he was sitting up, turned toward the door.

"What's the matter, boy? You hear somethin'?" B.J. sat up a little straighter himself, listening. Sparky was right—there *was* something. He jumped off the bed and crossed to the door. Sparky bounced up and down beside him, barking like crazy.

"Shhh," said B.J., "you're makin' such a racket I can't hear."

"This is incredible," said a voice only feet away. Angel's voice. There were a few grunts and groans. "What idiot did this?"

B.J. stood against the door like a rock. She sounded so close, she could almost be in the room with him. But, then, she almost was. The entrance to the attic, sealed off after B.J.'s death by his father, was at the back of Sean's closet. "We'll just leave all his junk up there and wall it up like he never existed," his old man said. "Just like he never was."

Sparky started throwing himself against the door. "Calm down, will ya?" B.J. grabbed Sparky's collar and pulled him back. "Maybe she's just cleanin' out the closet or somethin'. Sure, that must be it. She's just cleaning out the closet."

And then he heard it. Loud, clear, and unmistakable. The sound of splintering wood. For some reason, it made him think of the first shot fired in a war.

Chapter 5
The Battle of New Orleans

Angel stood at the bottom of the narrow, rickety staircase, peering into the dark. She wrinkled her nose in distaste. Something had definitely died up there. Something disgusting. Sean's stupid ghost, probably. "This better be worth it, that's all I can say," she muttered to herself as she began to climb, brushing cobwebs out of her hair and trying not to choke to death on the dust.

It had taken her ages just to find the entrance to the attic. She must have walked around the house half a dozen times, trying to figure out where it might be. Inside, she'd poked into every closet, looking for a trap in the ceiling.

Then it came to her. If the entrance to the attic wasn't in plain sight, then it must have been hidden deliberately, disguised as something else. Just as she'd once glued the binding of an old math book around her diary and stuck it on the shelf with her other books. Thank God she'd spent so much time thinking up new hiding places for her diary to keep it away from prying eyes: she might never have realized there was something funny about the size of Sean's closet.

After finding it, of course, it took her another eon or

two to break it open. Worth it? This attic had better be a big improvement on the room lived in by the Porterfields' maid, that was for sure. It had been such hard work to unseal the door that she'd almost been tempted to wait for Sean to come back to help her. Almost, but not quite. She hated the thought of having to thank him for anything. And, besides, this room was hers. She'd found it. She'd broken her nails and dirtied her clothes getting to it. She wasn't going to share it with anyone—least of all a demented ten-year-old.

Angel came to a stop at the attic door. *Please,* she silently prayed. *Please make it perfect. Make it the attic of my dreams.* She held her breath. *Don't worry,* she told herself. *It'll be great. It has to be. You deserve something really wonderful after all you've been through.* Very, very slowly, Angel turned the cracked glass knob. "Please don't be locked," she whispered. "Please." She pushed. Nothing happened. It must be stuck. Angel threw herself against it. There was a slight hesitation, and then it swung back with a groan. Her heart pounding, Angel stepped inside.

He'd been so certain that no one would ever discover the attic that it hadn't even occurred to him to lock the door. What for? By the time it finally did occur to him, when he heard Angel wrenching the false wall back from Sean's closet, it was already too late. *Key,* he thought, looking around in the gloom. *How am I supposed to know where the key is? Ghosts don't need keys. They walk through walls.*

Angel stood in the doorway for a few minutes, squinting into the room. "Oh, my God," she whispered. "I think something really *did* die up here." She took a step into the room and began to cough. *"Ooohyuk,"* she said in a choked voice, or something that sounded a lot like *ooohyuk* to him. "This is so gross. I'm going to be sick." She clamped a hand over her face and went straight to the window.

"Don't mind us," said B.J. as he pulled the yapping Sparky out of her way. "Just come right in."

"Air," gasped Angel. "I need air." A cloud of dust rose around her as she threw herself on the bed and opened the window a few inches.

"You don't need air," said B.J. "You need to go." He reached in front of her and slammed the window shut.

Angel coughed some more. "Doesn't anything in this house ever work?" She angrily shoved it up again.

"That must be why you fit in so well," said B.J. He banged the window closed again.

Angel started gingerly searching on the floor at the side of the bed. "Ugh," she groaned. "This place is so disgusting. . . ." Picking up a rotting sneaker with two fingers, she propped open the window. "I bet nobody's been up here for about a hundred years."

"Well, you bet wrong," snapped B.J. He would have flung the sneaker into the corner and shut the window one more time, but Angel had her face to the crack, taking gulps of fresh air.

When she was finally breathing again, she got up, peering around her uncertainly. "There must be a light," she said. She walked through Sparky as she groped along the wall for the switch.

B.J. was too surprised to react. It was the first time he'd realized how dark the room was, and the first time it had occurred to him that the light might work. He really *had* been dead a long, long time.

He was still just standing there, watching her, almost waiting to see what she would do next, when he heard a faint click. The dull yellow bulb in the middle of the ceiling went on.

Angel blinked. "I was right," she said softly. He couldn't tell from her voice whether she was happy or stunned. "It *was* a sort of bedroom."

"What do you mean, 'sort of'?" he demanded. "What do you mean, 'was'?"

Her eyes moved from the bed to the dresser; from the shelves in the alcove to the old oak desk; from the boxes in the corner to the pictures still hanging on the wall. Just as he couldn't tell from her voice whether she was happy or stunned, he couldn't tell from her expression whether she was pleased or horrified.

She shook her head, still taking everything in. "Look at all this junk," she said, putting her hands on her hips. "It'll take me forever to clean this out."

"Don't bother," said B.J. "There is no need, princess. You ain't stayin'."

She turned suddenly in his direction, looking straight at him for a second. Then her eyes fell on his jacket, thrown over the back of the chair beside him, for the first time. She made that sound again. *"Ooohyuk,"* said Angel, reaching out to touch the cracked leather. "I can't believe anybody actually wore this thing, it's so ugly." She lifted it as though she might throw it across the room, but instead she just stood there, staring at it, holding it in the air. Her eyes re-searched the room, but this time he could tell she was looking for something she hadn't already seen. Once again, she looked straight at him. It was almost as if she knew he was there.

If he'd had a heart, it might have skipped a beat. *What are you, nuts?* he asked himself. *There's no way she's startin' to see you.* Angel wasn't very young, very old, or very ill. And she was too self-centered and worried about her clothes to be psychic. *This chick don't see nothin' but herself.*

All at once, Angel gave herself a shake. "Well, this will be the first to go, that's for sure," she said, her voice suddenly loud.

B.J. watched in horror as she threw his jacket on the floor.

"First?" he repeated. "What do you mean, 'first'?"

Denise gave in even more quickly than Angel had hoped for. "All right," she said. "If you get the attic into a livable state, you can have it as your room. But you'll have to do it yourself. No one else is going to do it for you."

Angel had never claimed to be crazy about strenuous labor. She'd always tried to avoid anything that involved sweat or dirt—except cheerleading and tennis, of course—and she'd never seen any point in doing a thing for herself if there was someone else to do it for her. But she had to have the attic. It wasn't wonderful, and it was much more like a nightmare than a dream— but it had potential. It might never be the room she wanted, but it could be made into a room she could stand. At least she could fit all her furniture in it. At least the closet was large enough for most of her clothes. At least it had a view. Maybe she couldn't control anything else in her life, but she could control this. She could have a room where she could hide away and forget about how awful everything else was.

Angel threw her arms around her mother's neck. "Oh, of course!" she shrieked. "Of course I'll do it all myself. I wouldn't expect anyone else to do it."

Denise gave her a look. "Oh, of course not," she said. "What was I thinking of?"

"Wow!" Sean stopped dead in the doorway, staring at the attic as though it were Aladdin's cave. "This was his room, Angel. This was Billy's room!"

Angel finished tying a bandanna across her face so she could breathe without choking and shoved her brother out of her way. "I don't care whose room it was," she said, marching past him. "It's mine now." She dropped the boxes she was carrying with a thud.

Sean began to circle the attic slowly, touching everything as though it were made of gold—even the filthy old bed. "Wow," he kept saying. "Isn't this great? Wow."

"Just throw everything into the garbage," Angel directed. She shook out a large black plastic bag and illustrated what she meant by taking B.J.'s jacket and dumping it in. "Don't overfill them, though. We still have to get all this junk downstairs and out to the curb."

"Junk?" Sean swung around, something long and stringy and probably rat-chewed dangling from his hands. "This stuff's not junk. This stuff belongs to the ghost."

My god, thought Angel. *It's a leash. He is touching some disgusting, germy old leash with his bare hands.* "Not anymore it doesn't."

"Yes, it does," Sean protested. "You can't just throw it all out."

79

"Oh, no?" Angel scooped up a pile of comics and tossed them in after the jacket. "Just watch me."

"But, Angel, I think the ghost still lives here. I—"

"Ghosts don't live," snapped Angel, cutting him off. This was exactly the sort of thing she didn't want to hear. Yesterday, when she'd come in here, she'd had that feeling again. Not at first, not when she couldn't breathe or see, but once she'd gotten a little used to the place. That feeling that she wasn't alone, that there was someone else in the room. And then, when she'd picked up the jacket, she'd actually thought for a second that she could see something. Someone. A boy—a tall, dark boy, faint and miragelike, standing by the bed. *A trick of the light,* she'd told herself, and the image was gone. But the feeling had lingered on. "Ghosts are dead."

"But this one isn't, Angel. This one's an unquiet soul."

Angel pointed a bright yellow finger at him. She, for one, was wearing rubber gloves to avoid catching anything. Who knew what horrible dead things were moldering behind the boxes and furniture? "I'll 'unquiet soul' *you,*" she threatened.

Sean turned away and started going through the desk.

"I mean it, air brain," Angel said. "I'm only letting you help me to shut you up. If you're not going to do what I say, then you can go right back downstairs."

"Look at this!" Sean pulled a rectangle of blue paper from one of the drawers. "Look, Angel, it's a report card." He squinted at the faded writing. "'William Spatano, Grade Five,'" he read. "You see! His name *is* Billy!"

"*Was*," corrected Angel. "Now his name is on a gravestone somewhere, not on a report card." She threw another load of comics into the garbage. She really did wish Sean would stop acting like he believed in this dumb ghost—almost as much as she wished that she'd stop feeling as though he might be right.

Completely ignoring her, as usual, Sean pulled open another drawer. "Oh, wow! Will you look at this? Look, Angel! Just look!"

Angel looked. Now her brother was holding up something brown, stained, and definitely diseased. "Oh, excellent," said Angel. "That looks really exciting."

"It's a catcher's mitt," said Sean, sounding as though it really were exciting. "I bet Billy played ball."

"Oh, for God's sake." As carefully as she could, she knelt on the floor to see what was under the bed. "Every boy in the country plays ball except you." Sean was not just weird: he was about as athletic as a turnip.

Usually a remark like that would wind him up, but this time all he said was, "Yeah, but I bet Billy was good."

Angel dragged a pair of beat-up black boots and the dust of several ancient civilizations from under the bed. In one boot was a transistor radio and a key. In the other she found a watch and a switchblade knife. "Oh, sure," Angel said, turning the knife over in her hand. "He was good. He was a regular Boy Scout." She picked up the watch, a slim, gold woman's model. "I bet he stole this," she said. "Probably at knifepoint." She slipped the key into her pocket, in case it fit the door.

Anxious to get rid of as much as she could as fast

as she could, Angel moved through B.J.'s things like a whale through plankton. *Whop* went the pictures and the 1959 calendar. *Whop* went the things from the shelves. *Thump* went the shoes, and the sneakers, and the books. *Smash* went the mirror and the framed snapshot of a woman and a baby from the dresser.

While she threw things out, Sean went slowly and carefully through every item in the desk, one at a time, making a pile of what he wanted to keep. Angel decided not to waste any time arguing with him: she could dump what he'd saved later. The faster she cleared the room, the sooner she could start cleaning and painting—and the sooner this feeling would disappear.

And then Sean found one last thing stuck at the back of the desk, and he stopped being quiet. "Angel! Look at this!" When Sean got that excited, he sounded amazingly like Minnie Mouse.

She was never going to have children, Angel decided. Not only were they weird and annoying, but you couldn't get anything done with them around. And, besides, it might be genetic. She might end up with something like Sean. "Now what?" she demanded.

"This." He held out a yellowed newspaper clipping and the wallet-sized photo that had been tucked inside it. "It's *him*, Angel. It's Billy Spatano."

Curious in spite of herself, Angel went over to Sean. She stared at the creased black-and-white picture in his hand. A small short-haired dog with a pointed face was staring back at her from the seat of a large motorcycle. Behind the dog was a tall, dark young man—a boy, really—wearing a leather jacket and a surly expression. A shiver ran through Angel. It might have been a shiver of recognition—or of fear. "Ugh," she said, hoping Sean hadn't noticed that the photo had upset her. "He's a hood."

"And look at this," squealed Sean, holding the clipping up to Angel's face. "Mr. Stucker was telling the truth." The headline read, "Teen Killed Fleeing Scene of Crime."

Angel's eyes scanned the piece, picking out the words that mattered: *liquor store, robbery, gunfire, fatally wounded, motorcycle, pursuit, dead on arrival.* Suddenly, she could hear a voice. It was that voice again, the voice she sometimes thought she heard speaking softly in her ear. "This is my room," the voice was saying. "And I want you out." She looked up quickly, half-expecting to see the mirage of a boy standing in the doorway, but, of course, there was no one there. *It's the loneliness,* she told herself. *I'm having a nervous breakdown because of the loneliness. Loneliness and overwork.* "I don't have time for your nonsense," she said, pushing the article away.

"But this is so cool, Angel. Don't you think it's cool? It's just like on television."

Angel started hurling more things into the garbage. *"You're* just like on television," she replied. "Like Daffy Duck."

"It's going to be great," Angel told Lindy when she called that night. "It's almost like living in a tower." It was a slight exaggeration, she knew, but she hadn't said a *high* tower.

Lindy sighed. "I've always wanted to be able to look out my window and see the ocean," she said. "It's *sooo* romantic."

Angel wasn't sure that the murky waters of the beach below the bluff were what Lindy had in mind when she thought of looking out across the ocean, but it was certainly better than a view of the road. "It'll be a lot more romantic when I get the last of William J. Spatano's garbage out of it. You wouldn't believe the stuff I found. Talk about a blast from the past. This was more like a nuclear explosion."

"What about pictures? Did you find any pictures of him?"

Angel smiled. Leave it to Lindy to want to know what he looked like. Dopey or dead, Lindy didn't care as long as a boy was good-looking. "Yeah, Sean found a few."

"And?"

"And he looks like he was destined to die young. You know, that if he hadn't been killed robbing a liquor store, he would've been shot by the father of a pregnant teenager whose life was ruined by one night of lust on the back of a motorcycle."

"You mean he's cute."

Angel frowned in thought. "Not cute, exactly. More sort of attractive. Intense and no good, but attractive."

Lindy made a sound that combined a squeal with a sigh. "It's too bad there really isn't a ghost," said Lindy. "He sounds great."

Angel bit her lip. She'd decided not to tell Lindy that she was beginning to wonder about Sean's ghost. She didn't want Lindy to think she was losing her mind from loneliness, even if that was what she thought herself. "You wouldn't say that if you had to throw out his stinky old clothes," said Angel.

❈   ❈   ❈

Sparky moaned in his sleep as B.J., trying to find a more comfortable position for himself, pushed him to one side. The two of them were down in the basement, sitting on the washing machine, keeping out of Sean and Angel's way. So much for compromise. He couldn't even stay in his own room: he had to hide until Sean and Angel were in bed. B.J. moved out of the way of a dripping pipe. If he weren't already dead, spending hours in the damp cellar would have killed him by now.

B.J. had thought a lot about being dead when he was a kid. He'd dreamed about it. He'd planned it. When he died, they'd all feel bad. His old man, Danny, even Renee. Then they'd miss him. Then they'd be sorry. But he'd been wrong. They hadn't missed him, and they hadn't been sorry. Danny became a hero for risking his life to stop the hold-up. Renee had gone around telling everybody that she'd always known B.J. was a killer. And the old man had disowned him. "No son of mine," the old man had said. "I wish he'd never been born."

B.J. glanced nervously around as something scuttled under the dryer. He wished he'd never been born, too. At least that would solve all of his problems.

The other thing he'd imagined about being dead was that it would be peaceful. He'd be at rest. He hadn't been so sure about going to heaven and having wings and playing a harp and stuff like that— or going to burn and be poked with pitchforks in hell, if you listened to his father—but he'd figured he was going to be a lot happier when he was dead than he'd ever been when he was alive. Everybody'd be off his back. At last, they'd have to leave him alone. Wrong again. His death hadn't turned out to be peaceful.

Not only was he a restless spirit, but instead of being left alone, look what he had to deal with.

B.J. glanced up as footsteps pounded across the room above his head.

"This is the last time I'm doing this." Angel's voice—loud, bossy, and annoyed, as usual—echoed through the floorboards. "If you so much as take one comic back upstairs, you're history."

"But, Angel, I didn't—"

"How many times do I have to tell you?" she screeched. "It's junk. *J-u-n-k*. Leave it where it belongs."

"But it's not me," Sean whined. "I'm not putting the stuff back. It's Billy."

"Stop it!" she screamed. "I'm warning you, I don't want to hear one more word!" There was a shout of pain from Sean. "You'll be a ghost soon yourself if you don't cut it out, you little reptile." The front door slammed.

B.J. made a face at the ceiling. Angel Lister was what he got to deal with. She was the most selfish, spoiled-rotten girl he had ever known, and she was driving him nuts.

Every day this week, Angel had come home from school, changed into old clothes, wrapped a scarf around her hair, and marched up to the attic. She'd brought garbage bags and buckets of water. She'd brought cleaners, brooms, mops, sponges, rags, and scouring pads. She'd brought Sean. She'd filled plastic bag after plastic bag with B.J.'s things and dragged them out to the front of the house to await the Saturday morning pickup.

And every night this week, B.J. had gone out to

the garbage and brought stuff back. He couldn't believe it. She was taking over his room like a hostile army: quickly, and with no apology. She treated his most priceless possessions as though they were nothing. Out went the things he'd made in shop—the lamp and the box and the knickknack shelf. Out went his catcher's mitt and his old train set. Into the garbage went his mother's watch and the Harley parts bag he'd shellacked and kept filled with pencils. The cigarette lighter made out of a bullet casing that Danny had given him for his nineteenth birthday. His old key ring. The faded snapshot of a woman and a baby, "Mom and Billy, 1940"; the picture of him and Sparky the day he'd bought the Black Shadow; the notice of his death, "Teen Killed Fleeing Scene of Crime." It had taken him an hour just to find his jacket, buried under what any idiot could see was a priceless collection of Marvel comics.

Angel banged back into the house. "Come on, Sean," she was shouting. "We still haven't gotten that disgusting furniture outside."

That did it. At the rate things were going, he might as well be married, not dead. B.J. slid off the machine so quickly that Sparky almost fell off. *Disgusting furniture?* He'd give her "disgusting furniture." Wasn't it enough that she'd burned his blankets with the leaves?

"Mom said I can have it," Sean yelled back.

Angel came to a stop almost directly over B.J.'s head. "What for? You have furniture."

"For when I have friends stay over," Sean answered, sounding defensive. "Mom said it would come in handy."

Angel started to laugh. "Oh, give me a break. You've never had a friend stay over in your life. The only reason you want that garbage is because it belonged to your stupid ghost."

Sean stomped his foot. "So what? How would you like it if somebody threw all your things out?"

"I wish I could throw *you* out," said Angel.

"And I wish I could throw *you* out," said B.J. He drummed "The Battle of New Orleans" on the lid of the washer. It was a song he'd never liked that much, but he liked it now. No more Mr. Nice Guy, he decided. This was war.

Almost from the moment she discovered the attic, Angel had devoted herself to it as she had never devoted herself to anything before. Not even cheerleading. All through the long, lonely days at school, she'd kept herself going by thinking of her new room. How nice it was going to be. How cozy. How safe. How *hers*. She'd even begun to imagine that maybe, in time, she'd be able to have her own phone again, so that she wouldn't have to go into the living room closet to talk to Lindy with any privacy. Even though she'd had so much else to do—cooking, and housework, and homework, and looking after Sean— the first thing she'd done when she got home every day was work on the attic. She'd been determined to move in by the weekend.

Angel had grunted as she'd shoved the last of the plastic bags out the attic window. "There!" she'd announced to the empty room. "It's all out on the lawn. Every last comic and old sneaker. All of it!"

And then this morning, when she'd crossed the

lawn on her way to the bus stop, she'd noticed that the mountain of plastic bags had disappeared from the curb. *But this is Friday,* she'd said to herself. *The pickup isn't till Saturday.* A cold feeling she'd begun to get used to had rushed through her. Dropping her books on the lawn, she'd run back into the house and up the stairs. Sure enough, there it all was. After all her work. After all her hopes.

Maybe she really was losing her mind, but she'd known that it couldn't be Sean. Sean might rescue a few things—the ugly lamp, that revolting jacket—but he wasn't strong enough to carry all those bags up two flights of stairs.

"I'll get you for this!" she'd hissed. "I mean it, you punk! I'll get you for this!"

And that was when she'd heard him laugh, as clear as the sound of her own heart racing. For a second she'd been certain that if she wanted to, she would be able to see him. If she just turned in the direction of that cruel laughter . . . But she hadn't wanted to see him. She'd been crying too hard.

Well, we'll just see who has the last laugh, Angel had thought as she shut the door behind her and locked it with the key she'd found in the boot under the bed. She'd completely forgotten about the key until that morning. Then she'd realized that if she could lock the door, she might be able to stop Billy Spatano from bringing the bags back in again, even if she couldn't actually keep him out himself. Angel had smiled. "Yes," she'd said softly, "we'll just see."

"Hi! Angel? It *is* you, isn't it?

Angel looked up from heaving the last bag to the

curb to find herself staring blankly at a girl who'd stopped her silver racer on the other side of the pile of garbage. The girl was wearing a hooded, deep-purple sweatshirt and was smiling at her as though she knew her.

"It's me," said the girl. She pushed the hood from her head, revealing short blonde hair and six silver earrings. "Suze Adams. I'm in your history class, remember? I was just riding by when I saw you." She pointed to Angel. Her nails were incredibly long and as purple as her shirt. "I didn't recognize you at first. "I've never seen you in jeans."

Angel tried to hide her surprise. It had been so long since another human person had spoken to her in a friendly way that she was almost at a loss for words. "Suze." She nodded. "Of course I know who you are. You asked me about guillotining."

Suze laughed. It was a rich, warm laugh. Angel was suddenly aware that it was a laugh she heard often in the hallways of Midville High.

"That's right," said Suze. "And you said you hadn't really thought about it. And I said it wasn't worth losing your head over."

Angel found herself smiling. *Oh, my God,* she thought, *I didn't even realize she was making a joke.* It felt pretty good to be standing in the twilight, smiling.

Suze nodded toward the house. "So is this where you live?"

Angel followed her look. Her instinct was to say *Here? Oh, no, I don't live here.* Every time Angel thought about what might really happen if Silvia Samson and May Lewis wanted to be friends with her, she got as far as going for pizza or something, and then she stopped. She could never invite them to this dump. It would be like taking the queen of England to lunch at McDonald's. But there was no point in lying to Suze. She'd caught Angel red-handed, putting out the garbage. Unless she was the gardener, who else's house would it be? "Yeah. This is where I live."

"It's cool," said Suze, her eyes on the second floor. "It has atmosphere."

Angel gawked. "It does?"

"Yeah, it does." She turned back to Angel. "I'm not sure why, but I get a really strong feeling from that house." Suze shook her head. "I ride by here a lot, and I've always felt drawn to it, you know what I mean?"

Angel, who had no idea what Suze meant, nodded.

Suze shrugged. "I guess part of it's because it's haunted, but it doesn't scare me. It's like whatever haunts it is calling out to me."

"Haunted?" Angel repeated. "Really?"

"Uh-huh. That's why it's been empty for so long." Suze glanced back at the house. "I'm glad someone's living here now," she went on. "It's always felt so lonely."

Angel didn't know what to say. She was just getting used to feeling lonely herself. It had never occurred to her that a house could be lonely.

Suze pulled up her hood. "Well, I guess I'd better be going." She looked at her watch. "Gosh, look at the time. I'm going to be late if I don't hurry." She made a face. "Friday night," she said with a grin. Switching on her light, Suze began pushing the bike forward. "I'll see you, Angel. Nice talking to you."

"Yeah," Angel called after her. "See you!" She pulled her sweater around her. *Whatever haunts it is calling out to her?* There was no doubt about it, Suze Adams was even weirder than she'd thought. Angel frowned. Weird as Suze was, though, it really had been nice talking to her. The sky darkened, and a flurry of leaves fell to the ground. Angel stared after the disappearing figure on the silver bike. All at once she could see Suze Adams arriving home. Her mother and father were in the kitchen. The phone was ringing. It was for Suze. She couldn't talk long, though, because it was Friday night, and she was going out. Going out with all her friends. Angel gazed down Bluff Drive, picturing Suze and her friends at the movies. They were laughing and talking. They were touching and teasing each other. They couldn't agree on what to see. The boys started throwing popcorn. Someone put a piece of ice down Suze's back. She laughed so hard there were tears in her eyes. Angel blinked. The road was empty, the silver bike had vanished, leaves rustled across the ground. Angel turned back to the house, thinking about loneliness. There were tears in her eyes, too.

"That little brat." B.J. punched the wall with his fist. Sparky looked over. "I think I'd kill her if I weren't afraid I'd be stuck with her for eternity then."

He'd been pacing back and forth even since Angel had marched in after school, dumped two shopping bags in the corner, thrown all the stuff he'd salvaged out the window, and marched out again, locking the door behind her. She thought she'd won. She thought he'd have to give up now. But he hadn't given up. No siree bob. If she weren't so stubborn, she'd realize that he wasn't licked yet. He hadn't even started. But she was stubborn. She was the most stubborn person he'd ever met in his life—or his death. Stubborn? If Angel had been a boy, she would have been one of those boys who's always in trouble because he won't take orders. One of those boys who's always coming home with black eyes and a bloody nose because he never knows when he's beat.

B.J. shook his head. "Nah," he decided, "not killing. Killing's too good for her. Maybe I should shave her head. That'd get her."

He stopped by the shopping bags and peered in. They contained cans of paint, a paint tray, a roller, and brushes. He lifted out the cans by their handles. Tahitian Pink and Raspberry Melt.

"I'd like to melt her," B.J. muttered, throwing the Tahitian Pink across the room.

Sparky jumped.

"She's painting my room," said B.J. "Pink." Sparky looked at him. *"My room,"* he repeated. "Pink. *And* I'll bet she wants curtains. Pink curtains. In *my* room." He tossed the can of Raspberry Melt across the room, too. "I swear, Sparky, if they've got ruffles, I'm ripping them apart with my bare hands." Sparky waved his tail sympathetically. "I don't get it," said B.J. "I really don't get it." He ran his fingers through his hair and sighed. "This haunting stuff always works in the flicks."

93

Chapter 6
Leader of the Pack

Angel woke up as her mother left for the diner. She opened one eye, saw the time, and rolled over. *It's Saturday,* she told herself sleepily, *you don't have to get up for ages.* Coughing and popping, the van rumbled out of the driveway. *Saturday. There was something special about Saturday.* Still only half awake, Angel couldn't quite remember what was special about this Saturday. It wasn't Christmas . . . wasn't her birthday. . . . They weren't moving back to Lisson Park. . . . The blue eyes opened. *Moving.* That was it. It was the day she moved into her room. She looked at the clock again. Six-thirty. If she started now, the paint would be dry by this afternoon, and by night she'd be in, her curtains at the window and her fluffy pink rug on the floor. *My friends back home wouldn't believe this,* Angel thought as she threw herself out of bed. *Me, Angel Lister, excited about moving into an attic.* She wasn't sure she believed it herself. She hurried into her clothes and ran a brush through her hair. She looked around. "Good-bye, dungeon!" she cried. She felt happy. She really felt happy. Angel grabbed the old sheets Denise had given her to use as drop cloths and charged out of the room. She took the stairs two at a time, not thinking how much more surprised her friends back home would be if they knew that Angel Lister had gotten up at six-thirty in the morning to paint a room.

Angel froze in the doorway. Everything stopped. The song that was running through her head, the hum of the house, the crying of the gulls. The world. She couldn't hear, she couldn't move, she couldn't speak. All she could do was stare. *This is what hell must be like,* she thought. *This is hell.*

It was all back. Every record, every comic, every stupid motorcycle magazine, picture, T-shirt, and sneaker. Some of the stuff had been dumped in heaps on her beautiful waxed floor; some of it was still in its black plastic bags, piled one on the other like some sort of crazy tower. The leaning tower of rubble. For the first few seconds, that was all that Angel saw: things, junk. But then she felt it. *Him. If I look to my left, he'll be there,* she told herself. *If I just turn around, I'll see him. He can't hide from me now. If I just turn around.* . . She didn't know how she knew. She didn't know why. She turned to the left.

Dressed in grease-stained jeans, an old, torn, black T-shirt, and that disgusting jacket, a mangy old mutt curled up on his lap, he was sitting in the corner, leaning against the wall with a wise-guy smirk on his face, watching her through depthless black eyes.

"Billy Spatano."

Nothing showed in those eyes, but she could tell by the second it took him to speak that she'd surprised him. He'd thought he was still invisible.

"B.J.," he said.

Angel knew she should be frightened. Another girl

who suddenly discovered a long-dead young man in her bedroom—even if she'd been half-expecting him—would be frightened. She'd panic. Or scream. Or faint. Or burst into tears. She would almost certainly get out of the room as quickly as she could and never go back. But not Angel. She was too angry.

Why me? she wailed inwardly. *Why me?* Why was the world treating her like this? Didn't she already have more than her share of problems? Hadn't she suffered enough?

Angel's eyes traveled up and down Billy Spatano, from the scruffy boots and filthy jeans to the waterfall of hair that fell over his forehead and the cigarette tucked behind his ear; from the empty eyes to the insolent grin. *Terrific,* she thought. *Other families get demons and luminous ectoplasm, and we get James Dean.*

Angel clenched her teeth as anger swelled into rage. She'd had just about as much as she was going to take. She'd warned him. She'd told him yesterday that she'd had enough, and she'd meant it. The world had been pushing her around lately, but this was where it stopped, right here in this attic. There was no way she was going to let some dead hood interfere with her plans.

The silence stood between them like a wall of glass. Angel broke it. "Out!" she ordered. "I don't know what you think you're doing here, but this is my room, and I want you out!"

The dog sat up, but the boy didn't move. It was hard to tell from the expression on his face whether or not he understood English.

She raised her voice. "Out!" she repeated. She

took a step toward him. *"O-u-t. Comprende?* I don't want all your garbage in my room. I thought I made that clear." She put her hands on her hips. "And I definitely don't want you or that fleabag in it."

Very slowly, he got to his feet. He was taller than he'd looked in the picture; taller and broader. He jammed his hands in his jacket pockets and just stood there with an arrogant look on his face, as though she were the one who should apologize for being there.

"Can't you hear?" shouted Angel, "Can't you speak English?"

He nodded. "Yeah," he said, in the same deep voice she'd heard laughing yesterday. "I hear you just fine. I just ain't listenin', that's all."

Attitude. A ghost with attitude. Well, what did she expect? Casper? "You better start listening to me," Angel fumed. "Because I want you out, and that's all there is to it."

Even his smile was arrogant. "What're ya gonna do if I won't leave? Shoot me?"

Boy, did she wish that she could. "This is my room," she repeated, with a toss of her head. "And you don't belong here."

He pointed a finger whose nail was broken and rimmed with dirt straight at her throat. He grinned, but there was no humor in those black-hole eyes. "No, sweetheart, you've got it wrong. You're working under what we call a delusion here. This is *my* room, and the only thing that don't belong in it is you."

He was coarse, crude, arrogant, and dirty, and he was trying to intimidate her. She'd made it clear that she wasn't going to take any of his nonsense, but would he listen? No, he wouldn't listen. And why wouldn't he listen? He wouldn't listen because he was stubborn. He was coarse, crude, arrogant, dirty, *and* bull-headed. That was why. She could tell by the way his jaw set and the way he smiled, he was as stubborn as they came.

"And I'll tell you right now, honeybunch. You can keep throwin' my stuff out, but as fast as you get rid of it, I'm gonna bring it back."

Angel drew herself up to her full height. She raised her chin. Just because he was at least six inches taller than she was and had been dead since the fifties, he thought he could make her back down. But he was wrong. Wild horses, nuclear submarines, and the marines couldn't make her back down now.

"Out!" Angel reached for him, to pull him to the door, but her hand slipped through him as though he were air.

He smiled. She really hated that smile.

"It don't work like that, Miss Cheerleader."

Angel didn't even see him move. One second he was giving her that stupid, lopsided, God's-gift grin. The next, he had his hand around her wrist in a strong, hard grip.

"I can hold you," he whispered, "but you can't hold me." He winked. "Neat, ain't it?"

Because to touch him was to touch nothing, she couldn't kick him, she couldn't knee him, she couldn't simply push him away. Every time she pulled, he pulled harder, tugging her around the room as though he wanted to dance.

"Let go of me, you criminal!" Angel shrieked. "Let go of me right now!"

He started to laugh.

Laughing! The goon was laughing at her! He was dragging her around like a doll, and laughing at her! If there was one thing Angel hated more than not getting her way, it was being made fun of. No one made fun of her. No one. Never in her life had she wanted to hurt anyone—physically hurt someone and inflict untold pain—as much as she wanted to hurt Billy Spatano. No wonder he'd died young; they'd probably been lining up to wring his neck for years. Strengthened by fury, she finally managed to yank herself free.

She rubbed her wrist. For a spectral spirit, he had some grip. "Just what's so incredibly funny?" she demanded. "Somebody give you a mirror?"

"*You're* funny, that's what's so funny." He leaned against the open door, shaking his head. "How come you're not afraid of me?"

"Afraid of you? I'll give you 'afraid'!" She grabbed the nearest plastic bag and hurled it down the attic stairs. "You think I should be afraid of *you?*" She picked up a handful of magazines and threw them after it. "I'll show you who's afraid of you, you arrogant piece of toe-jam." She reached for the tacky wagon-wheel lamp.

It was definitely true; he could hold her. He could hold her very tightly.

The sudden feeling of his arms around her surprised her more than anything else he had done. Not just because she hadn't expected it, but because he felt so real . . . so close . . . so . . .

He lifted her off the ground as though it were she who was nothing.

"Put me down!" she screamed. "This minute! I mean it. Put me down!"

He dropped her on top of a filthy pile of comics.

The laughter stopped. "Let's just get one thing straight here, princess. This is my home, and I ain't goin' nowhere."

She struggled to her feet, brushing dirt and probably fleas from her jeans. "That's what you think," she said with every bit of venom she could muster. All at once she had a place to put all the hurt, confusion, and anger she'd been feeling since that cold winter night when her parents had first told them about the divorce. At last, her feelings had found their focus. She had something to hate as she had never hated anything before: William J. Spatano, deceased. She stamped her foot. "This is my room, and I'm not leaving."

He took a step toward her. "Oh, yeah?"

Angel had no idea what she thought she would do, but she took a step toward him. "Yeah."

Whatever might have happened, she was saved, not by the bell, but by a high, loud voice behind them.

"Billy! Billy, it's really you!"

They both turned at once. Angel hadn't heard Sean come up the stairs, and it was clear from the look on his face that Billy hadn't either. But there Sean was, still in his pajamas and looking rumpled, holding onto the doorjamb. He was so excited he almost glowed.

"I knew you were real, Billy," Sean squealed. "I told them. I knew it all along."

"B.J., not Billy."

Angel took advantage of the distraction provided by her brother to regain her composure. "Don't get yourself all wound up," she advised him. She returned her glare to the hoodlum before her. "Billy the Kid, here, isn't staying."

He glared back. "My name's not Billy, it's B.J."

She started kicking things out of her way. "I don't care if your name is Santa Claus. You're still out of here. Splitsville, man. Gone."

Sean didn't even glance at Angel. "You can come live in my room," he offered immediately. "I've got your bed and everything anyway. It'll be cool. It'll be like camp or something. I won't tell Mom, Billy. I swear I won't."

"B.J." He kept his eyes on Angel. "Thanks for the offer, but this is my room, and it's stayin' my room."

"You mean it *was* your room." Angel shook out one of the sheets and started to spread it over the floor. "Now it's *my* room." When she'd finished with that, she walked over to where the can of Tahitian Pink lay on its side and picked it up. She picked up the tray and the roller and the stirrer, too. She put them all on the sheet. He wasn't saying anything, but she knew he was watching her. She could feel those eyes. Slowly and deliberately, she opened the can. "And if you don't want all your precious garbage covered with paint, I suggest you get it out of my room and out of my way while you can," she said.

"Really, B.J.," Sean babbled. "I won't hurt you. Really. I want to be your friend."

B.J. said nothing.

"Tell him, Angel," Sean pleaded. "Tell him he can stay with me."

Angel, concentrating on filling the paint tray and not wanting to meet that dark gaze again, said nothing.

101

The silence grew. Longer. Deeper. More hostile. Filling up the room as though it would displace all the air. She knew that he was watching her—calculating, thinking, waiting. She knew that he knew that she knew. And she knew that he knew she was calculating, thinking, and waiting, too.

It was Sean who gave in first. "If no one's going to talk to me, I guess I'll get some breakfast," he said.

No one answered. No one looked his way.

"Don't move, B.J.," he ordered. "I'll be right back."

"I ain't budgin'," said B.J.

"You mean *yet,*" said Angel.

B.J. sat on the floor at the opposite side of the room from where Angel was furiously covering the wall in a color that reminded him of Pepto-Bismol, studying her while she worked. *How come she can see me?* he wondered. *What's changed?*

Angel slapped the roller against the wall so hard that B.J. ducked.

It had surprised him yesterday when he'd realized that she'd heard him laughing. And it had surprised him this morning when she'd burst into the room and he could tell she knew he was there. But it had surprised him even more when she'd turned around and looked right at him and spoken his name. *Geez,* he'd thought. *She sees me. She sees me clear as day.*

He took the cigarette from behind his ear and lit it, thinking. He knew that this awareness of him wasn't because of age, health, or any special powers. He blew a smoke ring in Angel's direction. And you could rule out artistic sensitivity, that was for sure.

She was the worst painter he'd ever seen. A blindfolded chimp would have her beat by a mile. *And* be a whole lot neater.

He shook his head as another spray of Tahitian Pink drifted across the room. "Why don't you try goin' a little slower?" B.J. suggested. "You know, use nice, easy strokes so it only goes where you actually want it." She was so bad that to prevent everything he owned from being speckled with paint, he'd had to cover the pile with one of her sheets.

Angel, lightly dusted with Tahitian Pink herself, rolled on. "I don't need you to tell me how to paint," she snapped.

"You sure need *someone* to tell you how to paint. You paint like a spray can."

"And you smell like the girls' room right after lunch. Do you have to smoke that thing?"

"Yes, I do. It happens to be one of the few pleasures I have left." He blew another smoke ring in her direction. "Especially since I met you."

Angel gave him a look as she dipped her roller in the paint tray. "What a shame it can't kill you."

One blue wall had almost disappeared. Along with quite a bit of the oak floor and molding. "You sure have a thing about pink," he said conversationally.

She pretended not to hear him.

"Now to me, having a pink room is like sleeping in medicine."

She banged the roller against the plasterboard again. "Then it's lucky you don't have a pink room, isn't it?"

"Gray," said B.J. "I could never figure out what was wrong with gray. My old man went crazy when I wanted to paint it gray, but I think it's very

103

soothing." He watched her move the ladder, slapping it into the wet wall. "You look like a girl who could use a little soothing."

"I look like a girl who could use a little peace and quiet." She was a pro, though, when it came to that look of contempt.

"I know it's hard t'believe, since you're paintin' everything else in sight, but you missed a spot in the other corner."

"Shut up."

"I just hope you've got enough turps to clean all this up when you're through."

"You really do come from the Ice Age, don't you?" She sneered at him over her shoulder. "You don't need turpentine for this paint, caveman. You just wipe it up with water."

He gave her one of his most charming smiles. "I guess it must've been invented with you in mind."

"Just like jail was invented for you."

It had always been a rule of his that you never hit a girl. Not ever. No matter how crazy she made you. Never. But it was a rule that Angel was already tempting him to break. *Just one. Just one in the kisser.*

He hadn't liked her from the start. The minute he saw her flounce out of the car and stalk across the lawn like Cleopatra checking up on how the slaves were doing, he'd thought, *Pain in the butt.* He knew her type—boy, did he know her type. She was one of those girls who have everything: looks, friends, popularity, money, parents who adore them. Everything. And they think they deserve it. They think nothing should ever go wrong for them. They think the world owes them a living, as his old man would have said. He still remembered them from school, strutting through the hallways like they owned the whole world, their laughter like knives. The type of girl who wouldn't give someone like him the time of day.

But he'd only disliked Angel before he and she had become better acquainted. Now that he was getting to know her so well, B.J. understood that he'd been wrong in thinking she was as bad as those girls in school. He'd done her an injustice. She was a million times worse. He didn't dislike her, he loathed her. Talk about a princess! Talk about thinking the world owed you a living! Angel thought the world owed her a ticker-tape parade, as well. She was the most stuck-up chick he'd ever met. Who could coexist with someone like her? He might be dead, but that didn't make him a saint.

Angel stretched to reach the top of the wall. If only he had a pea shooter. Then he wouldn't have to punch her, he could just land one spitball right on her pretty little rear.

Angel's voice, cold and sharp, interrupted his thoughts. "I don't know why you're just sitting around watching me," it was saying. "You've still got to get all your junk out of here. Today."

"And what if I don't?"

Her eyes were cold and sharp, too. "Then I do what I did to those moth-eaten old blankets. I torch it."

She would, too, the self-centered little brat. Maybe it was going to take him longer to get his room back than he'd thought. Longer, and a little more effort. But that was okay. He could handle that. If they were going to see who could tough it out longer, Little Miss Cheerleader was going to find herself out of her league.

Because, unlike her, he had all the time in the world.

"Just stop givin' me that look, okay? That look really drives me nuts."

"And what look would that be?" asked Angel Lister, her mouth in a scowl and her nose in the air.

"The one where you're the princess and I'm the guy who shines your shoes."

She stepped down to refill the paint tray. "Don't flatter yourself," she told him. "You're not good enough to shine my shoes."

Deck her. He really would like to deck her. Just once. Send her to the moon.

Footsteps sounded on the stairs. He could hear Sean's voice, fast and urgent, even before he was in the room. "So?" he was yelling. "So, have you decided? Have you made up your mind?" The door flew open. "Well?" Sean demanded. "I got all my stuff out of your dresser and your desk. Are you moving in with me?"

B.J. stood up, stretching slowly, turning up the collar on his jacket, watching Angel out of the corner of his eye. He'd read *The Man Without a Country* when he was in school. Now here he was, the man without a room. "Temporarily," he said at last. "Till her majesty here goes back downstairs."

"When hell freezes over," said Angel. She gave him a sugary smile. "And won't you be cold then."

He returned her smile. "That might be a lot sooner than you think, sweetheart. A lot sooner than you think."

Sean never shut up. All the while they'd lugged B.J.'s things downstairs, all the while he'd helped B.J. put it away, Sean had talked. He'd told him about school (it was okay, but he still hadn't made any friends). He'd told him what Mr. Stucker said about B.J. (that he was a murderer and a thief and his family had left town in shame). He'd told B.J. what his favorite foods were (chocolate, mashed potatoes, and cheese-and-peanut butter sandwiches). He'd told him about computers, videos, Nintendo, the space program, and pump trainers. You'd think the kid had never talked to anyone before. As fascinating as it all was—especially Mr. Stucker's stories about him—B.J. had been relieved when Angel had made Sean go downstairs for lunch.

He was sitting in the recess in the roof outside of Sean's window, recovering, when he saw the girl. She had blonde, cropped hair and was all in red—red leggings, red sweater, red basketball shoes. She glided up the driveway on a silver racer, hitting the horn. He wasn't used to girls who rode that way, or wore their hair so short, or dressed like that, but she was something. She was definitely something. B.J. leaned over the roof to get a better look. That was when he realized that he'd seen her before. Mainly he'd seen her riding past the house. The silver racer was new: she used to ride a black mountain bike. And she'd stopped sometimes, walked the bike up the front path, and just stood there, staring at the house, almost like she'd known he was in there. But that wasn't why he'd noticed her. It was her face—those round eyes, that full, wide mouth. If ghosts could dream, he'd known that he would dream about that face.

She crossed the lawn. She was coming to the house. It hadn't struck him before, but since the

Listers had moved in, the only other people who'd come to the house were the mailman and the newspaper boy. No visitors. No guests. No friends. But this girl wasn't selling Girl Scout cookies: she must be Angel's friend. When she disappeared under the roof of the porch, he climbed back inside and went to stand at the top of the stairs.

"Suze!" He could hear the surprise in Angel's voice. She was much more surprised to see Suze on the doorstep than she'd been to see him upstairs.

Suze's voice was the voice he would have imagined for her, clear and strong and warm. "I was just passing, so I thought I'd stop and say hello."

Angel wasn't going to invite her in. He could tell by the awkward silence. The little snob. This wasn't the sort of girl she used to hang out with in Lisson Park, and she wasn't going to invite her in.

When Angel finally spoke it was all in a rush. "Well, Suze . . . I . . . I'd ask you in, but I'm painting my room and—"

Suze's voice moved from the porch to the hall. "Painting?" she said. "Well, why don't I give you a hand?"

It was later, lying on his bed in Sean's room, listening to Angel and Suze laughing and talking upstairs, that he remembered the letters to Lindy about all the fun she was having; that he remembered the crying at night. Now he knew what had made Angel aware of him. Not age, not health, not ESP. Just lonliness.

Chapter 7
Who's Sorry Now

Angel was sitting on the floor of the living room closet, the door shut, the dim light on and the telephone on her lap. Even though Denise, of course, was at the diner, Sean might barge into the house at any minute. Sean or B.J. At least being in here made her feel like she had some privacy.

"Oh, Lindy, I'm so glad you finally called," she said, a note of accusation in her voice. "It's been ages since I heard from you."

Lindy giggled. "I guess I'm just not really into letter writing," she admitted. It wasn't exactly an apology. "I mean, it takes so long . . . and anyway, I've been too busy to write. I mean, there's so much happening. I don't know when you find the time."

"I don't know myself how I manage," replied Angel. There was no way she was going to admit to Lindy that she had plenty of time for writing letters. She had enough time to write *War and Peace*.

"And, anyway, I really prefer talking on the phone," said Lindy. "It's so much more personal."

And more expensive, thought Angel. Denise allowed them one call to Marshall a week, Saturday cheap rates, and she kept her eye on the clock the whole time. It was probably just as well that Marshall was hardly ever in. But Lindy, of course, still lived in a world where a long-distance phone call wasn't considered a major luxury.

"So, tell me what you've been doing," Lindy went on. "Met any cute boys? Go to any good dances? Bought any cool clothes? What about parties? Allison Fletcher's planning a big masquerade for Halloween. It's going to be fantastic. . . ."

Angel moved a boot out of her back and tried to make herself comfortable while Lindy proceeded to tell her how *she* was doing. What cute boys she'd met in the last twenty-four hours, what great dances she'd been to, what new clothes she'd bought, what she was going to wear to Allison Fletcher's masquerade . . .

While Lindy described her costume and how much it would cost in minute detail, Angel's mind began to wander. There was a certain sameness to her conversations with Lindy that she'd never noticed when they were together. Now, though, they were all beginning to seem like one conversation—except that the names of the boys, themes of the dances, and colors of the clothes changed from one to the next.

The sudden intrusion of a voice that wasn't Lindy's interrupted her thoughts. "Don't tell me, let me guess," it was saying. "You're talking to Miss Shop till You Drop."

Angel looked over with a scowl. B.J. was sitting across from her, one of Denise's floral scarves dangling next to his head. She hated it when he suddenly appeared like this. Which was exactly why he did it. It was part of his plan to wear her down. And he'd been at her magazines again. She could always tell when he'd been reading her magazines, because he'd have a new phrase or suddenly want to talk about low-fat diets.

"Shut up," she hissed.

B.J. laughed. "Don't ya wanna know how I know?" He winked. "I know because you never get a word in edgeways. You just sit there listenin' to her tell you the same old garbage again."

"Shut up, I said." Angel tried to concentrate on what Lindy was telling her about stretch pants.

"What?" asked Lindy, interrupting herself. "Did you say something, Angel?"

Angel kept her eyes on her feet, ignoring B.J.'s knowing, wise-guy grin. "I said they sounded cool."

"I don't know why you waste your time with this dizzy chick."

B.J. stretched his legs, one filthy boot leaning against Angel's arm. She tried to move away as Lindy went on to discuss patterned tights, but there wasn't really anywhere to move to. It wasn't a big closet.

"Whatever happened to that Suze girl?" asked B.J. "The one who helped you paint your room. You two were gettin' on like a house on fire."

Oh, how she wished she could kick him. "Mind your own business," she whispered.

"Me?" asked Lindy. "Angel, are you talking to me?"

"But you liked her," B.J. insisted. "How come you never invite her over?"

"Is there someone with you?" asked Lindy.

111

Angel gave him a look. "You mean *you* liked her." Silvia Samson and May Lewis might not find Suze Adams attractive, but William Joseph Spatano definitely had. He never shut up about her.

"You liked her, too," he insisted. "Don't tell me you didn't." He nodded toward the receiver. "Suze's a lot more interestin' than the Mad Shopper. All she ever talks about is boys and clothes. And that *laugh*!" He rolled his eyes. "It's enough to drive anyone nuts."

"You're enough to drive anyone nuts," snapped Angel. "And stop reading my mail!"

"Angel, answer me!" Lindy sounded annoyed. "Who are you talking to?"

"Don't get all worked up just because I'm right," said B.J. "You should call up Suze and ask her to do somethin' with you. You've gotta get out more, make some new friends."

That was just what she needed, advice on her social life from the living dead. "I can't get out more, can I?" She was going to start shouting in a minute. "I have to take care of Sean."

"So have her come here. We could all watch a video together."

Angel sighed. *Oh, great,* she said to herself. *That's a cozy thought.*

"Angel? Angel, are you there? What's going on?"

"It'd be cool," B.J. insisted. "Maybe we could get *The Wild One* out. I haven't seen it in years."

"I live with it, I don't have to watch it."

"Angel? Angel, *who* are you talking to?"

What was the point? Lindy had nothing to say to her, she had nothing to say to Lindy, and B.J.

112

wouldn't let either of them say anything anyway. "My mom's just come in, Lindy," lied Angel. "I'm going to have to hang up."

B.J. put on a mock-apologetic face. "Oh, please," he begged, already on his feet and fading through the door. "Don't let me disturb you."

Angel stared at the place where he'd been.

"I really don't know what's with you lately," grumbled Lindy. "You're always so distracted when I call."

As soon as supper was over, Angel left Sean watching television and went to her room. "He'd better not be in there," she muttered as she stomped up the stairs. "He'd just better not be, that's all."

Angel stood in the doorway and sniffed. The room smelled of Chica!, her favorite cologne; Summer Morning, her favorite body powder; Potpourri, her favorite body spray; and, very faintly, B.J. Spatano's cigarettes.

"Stop it!" Her eyes searched the room. "I mean it, Spatano. I want this to stop." The bedspread was mussed up, her magazines were scattered over the floor, and the things on her dresser had been opened and moved around—but there was no sign of B.J. "Do you hear me?" she shouted. "I know you've been in here again." And she knew why.

Angel started straightening up, checking her pillow for traces of Brylcreem. She knew the way his limited mind worked. This was guerrilla warfare. Because of the room. Angel dusted boot prints from her pink spread with a sigh. Like he really had any use for it. Like he had a life. He thought that if he bothered her enough, that if he harassed and annoyed her every minute of the day and night, she would give in. That eventually she would say, "Okay, you win, it's not worth it, you take the room."

But he was wrong. She wasn't backing down that easily.

Angel started picking up the magazines. She could take him messing up her room. She could take him going through her things. She could even handle his constant bickering—after all, she'd lived with Sean for ten years, she was used to it. What she couldn't stand was his fascination with her life. *Who d'ya hang out with? Who d'ya talk to? Why don't ya ever go out?* But of all the aspects of her life that fascinated B.J., Suze Adams seemed to fascinate him the most. Angel dumped the magazines into their rack. She didn't like to think about Suze Adams.

The truth was they'd had such a good time the Saturday Suze stopped by out of the blue that Angel had actually forgotten how strange Suze was, and how different from the friends she was used to.

Suze had been full of stories and gossip that made her laugh. By the time Suze had left that afternoon, they'd even been talking about getting together again. But then had come Monday morning, back in the real world. Angel had been getting her things out of her locker when she'd seen Suze coming toward her. Suze had smiled and waved. Angel had been about to rush up to Suze, to pick up where they'd left off, when she'd spotted Silvia Samson and May Lewis right behind her. The smile had frozen on her face; her hand had fallen to her side.

All she'd been able to think of was that if Silvia and May thought she was friends with Suze, they would never be friends with her. She would never join the cheerleaders. She would never be invited anywhere. She would never fit in. Suze had slowed down as she neared Angel's locker, opening her mouth to speak. And Angel had looked right through her. She'd known she shouldn't, but she hadn't been able to help herself. She'd looked right through her, banged the door shut, and strutted past Suze Adams just the way that Silvia Samson and May Lewis strutted past her.

Angel started cleaning up the mess on her dresser. No, she didn't want to think about Suze Adams. And she certainly didn't want to discuss her with B.J.

Even someone whose life is as much fun as peeling two tons of potatoes can have a best part of the day, and at last Angel came to hers. Hers was the hour before bed. Her chores over, her homework done, that was the hour that she spent with Gavin— even if only in her mind.

I think I'd die without this to look forward to, she told herself tonight, as she told herself every night. And just as she did every night, she kissed the gold heart she wore around her neck, the locket Gavin had given her when she'd left Lisson Park, as a token of his undying love. Then she took his photograph in its silver, heart-shaped frame from its home beneath her pillow and put it on the desk, where she could see it while she wrote. After Gavin was in place, Angel got out her best stationery, the box her mother had given her the previous

115

Christmas, with stars and angels around the border. Then she took out her pink pen and laid it beside her writing paper. She lit a candle and put her and Gavin's song on the tape deck. She closed her eyes and tried to pretend that he was with her, that she could feel him and see him and hear his voice.

"Y'know, you really should get some real music, Angel."

Angel opened her eyes.

"I know you've got this mental block about Elvis, but at least get some Conway Twitty or Chuck Berry, something that rocks. Even the Shirelles are better than this crap."

"Watch your language."

"Sorry." He leaned over her shoulder. "Even the Shirelles are better than this animal excrement."

"Go away." She kept her eyes fixed on Gavin's handsome face, smiling at her from his Corvette. Gavin's wide, bright smile was nothing like B.J.'s crooked, smart-aleck grin. Gavin smiled to show off his excellent teeth. B.J. only smiled when he thought something was funny. Most of the time, that seemed to be Angel. She picked up her pen.

B.J. picked up the photo. He slid onto the corner of the desk, shaking his head. "I just can't believe it. This is the guy who won the heart of our princess. A jerk who wears pastel sweatshirts with someone else's name on them."

She grabbed the photograph out of his hand. "Don't get your germs all over that."

As soon as she put the picture back, he picked it up again. "This is the guy who gave you that chintzy locket, right?"

She put her hand over the locket, which was not, perhaps, as gold as she had originally thought. She'd had to stop wearing it in the shower because it had a tendency to peel.

"He's the same one who sends you those postcards with the pictures of flowers on the front, yeah?"

How was a girl supposed to concentrate on love when she was so overwhelmed with hate? "They're his mother's notecards, if you must know. They happen to be very expensive. They come from the Metropolitan Museum of Art in New York City."

"I don't care if they come from Boogie Eddy's in Nashville," B.J. said. "They're still pictures of flowers." He leaned so close she could smell a faint trace of Chica! "How come this joker can't ever write you a whole letter?" He closed his eyes and put one hand over his heart. "'Dear Angel of Mine'," he recited in a squeaky voice, "'I really miss you. Everyone says hello and wants to know when you'll be back. I have to go now. Love, Gavin.'"

Angel stared down at her notepaper. She didn't know why Gavin never wrote her a whole letter, or why his notes were getting briefer and more impersonal as the weeks went by. Or why he seldom phoned. She'd decided it must have something to do with being a senior. Because he was so busy.

She ripped the picture away from B.J. again. "How many times do I have to tell you, you barbarian? Keep out of my things."

He held up his palms as though fending her off. "Okay, okay, don't get yourself all worked up. I'm just tryin' to help, that's all. You should listen to your old Uncle B.J., though. The boy's another waste of your time. Why you mess around with these lame-os when you could be hanging out with Su—"

"He is not a waste of time." Angel slammed the frame back on the desk. "He is the man I love."

B.J. made a sound that Angel had once believed could only be made by a pig. "That ain't no man, sweetheart. That's a boy."

"Young man," snapped Angel, trying to think of something to put on the paper besides *Dearest Gavin.* Not only could she not explain why Gavin wrote so little to her, she couldn't explain why every night it seemed to get harder and harder to find something to write to him.

"You can't be for real." He snorted with laughter. "How could you love *him?* I mean, I know you're a drag, sweetheart, but this guy looks about as interesting as a bowl of instant vanilla pudding."

"He is not, you cretin."

B.J. grinned. "Yeah, maybe you're right. Maybe he isn't as interesting as instant pudding."

Angel flinched. A traitorous voice deep inside her was agreeing with the delinquent. This voice was reminding her that it was no longer easy to recall the funny, intelligent, and fascinating things she knew that Gavin must have said and done. This voice was reminding her that Gavin's kisses had been about as thrilling as a bowl of instant pudding, too. *B.J.'s right,* this voice was whispering, *the most interesting and thrilling thing about Gavin is that everybody else wants to go out with him.* She shut out the voice. She'd buy her clothes in the five-and-ten before she'd admit it might be right.

Recovering herself, Angel rallied her forces of scorn. "And this from a creature with the IQ of an amoeba."

He took up the photograph yet again, pretending to study it for clues.

You couldn't even insult him. He was so stupid he probably didn't know what an amoeba was.

"Come on," he urged, "you can tell me. What is it you love about Mr. Joe College here?"

Angel sneered. "Like you really have to ask . . . Gavin's only on the varsity football team—"

"Oh, right, princess. That's a real testament to his character and charm." He poked her with his elbow. "Anyway, I always liked baseball better. It's got more soul."

"Which is more than can be said for you."

He put his lips to her ears. "I've got a soul," he whispered. "It's just that it's tormented."

She concentrated on Gavin, trying to remember what she loved about him. "And he has his own Corvette —"

"Nah." B.J. shook his head, looking as though he'd just tasted something sour.

She wanted to shove the picture in his face. "What do you mean, 'nah'? He does too have his own Corvette. What do you think he's sitting in? A Volkswagen?"

"I meant, nah, I wouldn't want a Corvette. I always thought that if I was going to get a car—not that I would, you understand, I love my bike—but if I was, I'd get a pink Cadillac."

Talk about wasting your time! Why did she let

119

herself get involved in talking to him? It was worse than trying to have an intelligent, adult conversation with Sean. She slid her chair over. "Who cares what you thought? You're just a cheap punk!" She laid her head on the desk. "This is incredible," she said to an invisible audience. "Just incredible. Leather jackets . . . Elvis Presley . . . pink Cadillacs . . . I feel like I'm trapped in an episode of *Happy Days.*" She looked up at B.J. "Or *Unhappy Days,*" she amended.

B.J. flipped the picture face down. "So that's it? You love this clown because he wears shoulder pads and drives an expensive car?"

She finally met his eyes. "For your information, Mr. Pink Cadillac, not only is Gavin Spencer Smythe the best linebacker in the history of Lisson Park, but he's probably going to study business at Harvard and be a vice president by the time he's twenty-four."

That stupid smile returned. *"Study it?"* He was looking as though she'd said something good. "What's t'study? Why doesn't he just do it?"

Airhead. He was an even bigger airhead than she'd thought. "Oh, forget it, will you? How could someone like you understand? The only things you understand are gang fights and motorbikes."

"Cycles. And anyway, for your information, Miss Queen of the Prom, I was going to own my own business someday, too. Y'know, a bike shop or a garage, somethin' like that."

She looked at his hands, square and thick and never clean. The hands of a mechanic and the mind of a moron. "You know, it's really lucky for you that you're dead, or I'd probably wind up killing you."

He tapped a finger on her stationery. "Well, you're still alive," he told her softly. "So I'd watch my step, if I was you."

Sean squinted through the eyepiece, pointing the telescope over the bluff to where the sky was wide and high. "I got this for my birthday in May," he was saying, "but, you know, with moving and everything, I haven't really used it much. That's why it's so cool that I can set it up outside my window like this." He moved over and passed it to B.J.

"I don't know about this," said B.J.

"Don't be afraid," said Sean. "It's just like looking through glasses."

B.J. approached the telescope gingerly, giving Sparky a little shove to get him out of the way. B.J. was good with carburetors and stuff like that, but a telescope was something new.

"You see Jupiter?"

How would he know? This was nothing like looking through glasses. "I don't think so." He wasn't sure what he was seeing. There were colors and motion he'd never expected. And then, all of a sudden, the sky seemed as close as Connecticut, the ends of the galaxy as real as the water below the bluff. "I— Geez, this is really somethin'."

"Jupiter is sort of creamy white. You see it?"

"I think so. . . ."

"Okay. Now, you see those tiny little dots around it?"

B.J. nodded. He could just make out four small specks, so faint they might not exist. "I've never

121

seen anything like this before," he said softly. "I guess I was sick the time my class went to the planetarium."

"Those are the moons. The moons of Jupiter. Aren't they neat?"

"They're neat," B.J. agreed. "They're very neat. It's kinda nice to know Jupiter's not alone up there."

"My old telescope wasn't this good," Sean informed him. "It was better than binoculars, but it wasn't like this. My mom helped me pick it out. You want to see some double stars?"

"Sure," he answered, but he didn't move from the scope. Before tonight, he'd never even heard of double stars. He thought stars, like people, were pretty much by themselves. But Sean said no. Sean said most stars had companions.

"There's a good double star in the Big Dipper," said Sean. "Or maybe you'd like to see another galaxy." He pointed excitedly into the dark. "You want to see Andromeda? It's really cool, B.J., it's much bigger than the Milky Way. And you know how far it is? It's 2.2 million light-years away. Isn't that great?"

2.2 million light-years. Farther than Connecticut. He slowly tracked the telescope across the sky. Somehow, when he was alive, he'd never paid much attention to things like moons and stars. Except, maybe, when he'd walked along the beach by himself on a dark night, feeling small and alone. Then he'd noticed them—and wished that he could just float free, straight into the sky.

"What's red?" asked B.J.

"If it's really bright, it's probably Mars."

B.J. turned to Sean. "I can't believe this has been up there all the time, and I never even thought about it."

"I knew you'd like it." Sean's face was as bright as the moon. "Didn't I tell you you'd like it?"

B.J. smiled. "Yeah," he said. "You told me." His eyes scanned the sky, trying to make out the constellations Sean had shown him: the giant hunter and the raging bull. "How'd you get interested in this? Your dad?"

"My dad?" Sean's smile disappeared. He moved over and pressed his eye to the telescope, making adjustments in a careful way. "No, not my dad."

B.J. watched the side of Sean's face, taut with concentration, pale in the darkness, searching for a galaxy 2.2 million light-years away. He should have kept his big mouth shut. He should have realized that since the Listers had moved in, Sean had only talked to his father a couple of times and then just long enough to say that he was fine and school was okay. It was funny, really. You always thought you were the only one.

"Your dad's not into astronomy, uh?"

Sean looked over. "My dad likes fishing and stuff like that."

B.J. leaned back against the window ledge. "So you're not exactly birds of a feather, right?"

Sean made a face. "I don't think we're even both birds." He moved away from the telescope, sitting down beside B.J. "One time he took me fishing with him. You know, it was supposed to be one of those father-son weekends?"

123

B.J., who didn't know, nodded. He'd been reading a lot about "male bonding" in Angel's magazines, but it wasn't something that had existed when he was a boy. Not with his old man. His old man had never taken him anywhere if he could help it. He'd taken Danny places, but not him. Didn't want to be embarrassed. Didn't want to be stuck talking to him. "That sounds cool." Sparky came over and stretched across his legs.

"It wasn't cool." Sean edged so close that B.J. had to put an arm around him to stop him from coming out the other side. "It was horrible. I fainted when he tried to show me how to gut a fish."

B.J. laughed. "No kiddin'?"

"It was awful. He was so humiliated he told his friends I'd had an asthma attack."

B.J.'s laughter rustled through the dark. "For real? He told them you had asthma?"

Something like a smile returned to Sean's face. "Uh-huh. And then, you know what? Then he got mad at me because everyone wanted to know where my inhaler was if I had asthma."

B.J. held up a hand. "Let me guess. Then your dad said it was your fault, because you'd forgotten to bring it along."

Sean looked at him like he was a mind reader. "That's right. That's what he did. He said he'd told me to bring it, but I'd still forgotten. How did you know?"

B.J. searched for the space in the sky where Jupiter had been. "My old man was a little like that. Hunting was what he liked, though. Guns." He made a face. "Me, I can't stand the sight of blood.

124

It's one of those things that should stay where it was put, is what I think."

Sean laughed.

B.J. gave him a punch. "Now what's funny?"

"That's exactly what Angel says about you: that you should stay where you were put."

"Oh, yeah? Is that what Angel says?" He was happy enough to get the conversation away from fathers. "What else does she say?"

Sean shrugged. "Oh, you know Angel. She just likes to complain all the time."

"Geez, does she!" Even his stepmother, Renee the Nag, hadn't griped as much as Angel. "I can't figure it out, though. What's she so unhappy about?"

Sean gave him a look. "Everything. She hates Midville. She hates school. She hates the house. . . ."

"My house! She's lucky I let her stay." B.J. flicked a twig over the roof. What a girl. She wasn't even here right now, and he wanted to deck her. She went around mooning over a drip like Gavin with his smug smile, his fancy car, and his insincere little notes about missing her, when the chances were he already had another girl. And she had the nerve to hate *his* house.

"I wouldn't take it personally," said Sean. "I mean, she's never really liked me much, and now she's not too keen on Mom, but we don't let it bother us."

"Your mother? She doesn't like your mom?" He knew they had fights, but mothers and daughters were always fighting—it was no big deal. Denise wasn't around enough to get on your nerves.

125

Unlike some people. "What's not to like about your mom? She has a tendency to ride the clutch, but otherwise she's cool."

Sparky rested his chin on Sean's legs. "She's a waitress. Angel can't stand waitresses. She says they're common."

"I've always liked waitresses," B.J. said. How many wee, wee hours had he sat in all-night diners, talking to someone named Peg or Barb about the weather and their problems and how someday they might go to Florida and live near the beach? "I had some good friends who were waitresses."

Sean held his hand out for Sparky to lick. "Don't let Angel hear you say that. She hates you more than anything else."

"At least the feeling's mutual," B.J. replied.

"She isn't really that bad," Sean said seriously. "Sometimes she can be a lot of fun. Mom says it's just that Angel's upset about the move and everything." His voice went to a whisper. "Mom says it's really because of the divorce. You know. She says Angel's having a hard time getting used to it."

B.J. stared up at the starry sky. Yeah, he knew. He'd had a hard time getting used to his mother's death, and to Renee, and to the fact that his old man only cared for Danny. Maybe he'd never gotten used to any of it; maybe that was why he was still here, all these years later, watching the sky.

"Look!" Sean pointed over the roof of the Morgens' across the street. "It's a shooting star."

B.J. looked, but he was still thinking about Angel. Most of the time just the sight of her flouncing up the road like Cleopatra made him want to throw her in the Sound. But every now and then, he'd see her coming from the bus or sitting staring out the window, looking all alone, and instead of seeming like Cleopatra, she reminded him of himself. "Maybe I should get to know her a little more," said B.J., almost thinking out loud. "Maybe if I understood her better, we could work things out."

Sean looked at him in surprise. "Who are you talking about?"

"Angel."

Sean shook his head. "I wouldn't bother if I were you. I've lived with Angel for ten years, and I don't understand her. I just try to stay out of her way."

"But I can't stay out of her way," B.J. protested. "She's in my room."

"Forget it," Sean said, going back to the sky. "I know you can't die again or anything, but you don't want to get her really mad."

B.J. smiled at the moon. "Don't worry about me. I can handle Angelina Lister."

Surprisingly enough, Angel had almost started to look forward to Sundays. It was the one day Denise had some time to spend with them, because she closed the diner after lunch. It probably just showed how desperate Angel was—she wouldn't have been caught dead hanging out with her mother and brother in Lisson Park—but she had to admit that they usually had a nice time. They might go for a drive, or to a movie, or pick up a pizza and a video, or even just play a game together.

Tonight, however, Angel didn't really feel like hanging out. She sat on the sofa next to her mother, but though Denise was watching television, Angel was staring at the screen with a glazed expression, her mind at least 2.2 million light-years away. Tonight, all Angel could think about was William Spatano.

How could you murder someone who was already dead? That was the problem. Scowling at the thought of him, Angel readjusted herself on the couch. "No wonder he's still around," Angel muttered out loud. "He's even too stubborn to stay dead."

Denise looked over. "Did you say something, honey?"

Angel met her eyes, trying to look innocent. Denise had begun watching Angel closely. It seemed like every time she turned around or looked up, she found her mother staring at her with a worried expression. And Denise had started to catch her talking to B.J. "What was that?" she would ask. Or, "Who were you talking to just now?" Or, "Angel, did I hear you yelling at someone in you room?" And then she'd give her a funny look. The other night, Denise had actually tiptoed halfway up the attic stairs before B.J. had said, "Shhh, stop snapping at me. I think I hear your mom."

It was hard enough not to get caught talking to B.J. without Denise sneaking around like a spy. He was always talking to her. Teasing her about cheerleading. Goading her about Gavin and Lindy. Calling her sweetheart. She'd told him a million times that her name wasn't Sweetheart, but all he said was, "Well don't tell anybody, *sweetheart*, but it shouldn't be Angel, either."

"And what should his be?" Angel mumbled. "King Kong?"

"Honey?"

Angel glanced over. Her mother was giving her that funny look.

"Did you say something?" asked Denise. "Did you want to change the show?"

"Oh, no," Angel answered quickly. "Oh, no, this is great." She set her eyes on the screen, wishing she knew what was going on.

And that was another thing. She couldn't even watch a movie without William Joseph Spatano flopping down next to her and complaining. "I always liked Groucho," he'd say. "Groucho and Jackie Gleason." Then he'd give her that stupid smile. "But I figure you're more the *My Little Margie* type."

"Angel," Denise was saying. "Angel, is something wrong?"

Wrong? What could be wrong? Last night he'd even had the nerve to tell her how to cook. "I'm just tryin' to give you some pointers," he'd told her. "You cook like a mechanic."

"And *you* are a mechanic," Angel said.

"Who's a mechanic?"

Angel jumped. Denise was looking at her like she'd turned green or something. "This is a pretty good movie, isn't it?" Angel asked brightly, hoping to change the subject.

"Angel Lister," Denise said, real concern in her voice. "I want to know what's wrong with you. You're sitting there, thumping around, talking to yourself. . . ." She ran a hand through Angel's hair. "Now, answer me."

Angel stared into her mother's troubled brown eyes. Should she tell her? Denise had gone nuts when she'd discovered all of B.J.'s things in Sean's room. She'd started screaming about his obsessive behavior, and being at her wit's end, and not having enough problems without having to have a son who believed in ghosts.

"Angel," said Denise. "I asked you a question. Who's a mechanic?"

On the other hand, if she told her mother the truth and managed to convince her, then they'd have to move. Angel cleared her throat. She took a deep breath. "B.J. Spatano."

Denise was smiling at her in an encouraging way. "Who?"

"B.J.," she repeated. "William Joseph Spatano."

The smile grew smaller as Denise's eyes grew wider. "Are we talking about Sean's ghost?"

"Who else?" Angel asked. "No one interesting ever comes here."

Denise leaned against the sofa as though she might collapse. "Are you saying that you believe in this ghost, too?"

Angel nodded. "He's real, Mom. It isn't just Sean being weird. B.J. Spatano exists."

"And you've seen him?"

"Seen him?" Angel rolled her eyes. "I can't get rid of him."

"And you've talked to him?"

"He never shuts up."

Denise closed her eyes for a second. "I don't know," she said, her voice choked with worry, "maybe I have been wrong about some things. I never expected you kids to react like this to the divorce. These fantasies . . . these hallucinations . . ."

Angel touched her shoulder. "But they're not fantasies and hallucinations, Mom. I told you. He's real. And he's a real pain, too."

Denise opened her eyes. "Honey," she said, as though Angel hadn't said a word. "Honey, since when have you believed that this house is haunted? Since the diner opened? Since you started school?"

"No, of course not." Angel sighed in exasperation. Now what was Denise getting at? "Just since that creep William Joseph Spatano started giving me such a hard time about taking over his room."

Chapter 8
Fool Number One

Really, Angel was thinking as she wrapped up Sean's sandwich, *who would want to be a mother? The pay's lousy, and the hours are worse.* The day hadn't even started yet, and already she'd put a wash in the machine, fixed breakfast, made the lunches, and found Sean's left sneaker under the sofa cushion— where, she was sure, Sparky Spatano had hidden it out of spite. She looked at the clock. If she didn't hurry, she was going to miss her bus. That was all she needed. School was bad enough without having to walk to it.

"Your lunch is on the counter," she said to Sean as she put on her jacket.

Sean didn't look up from the book he was reading while he inhaled his cereal. "Okay."

"And you have your homework and everything, right?"

Sean nodded. "Yeah, sure."

"And you won't forget to lock the front door when you leave?"

"Uh-huh."

"And you're keeping your eye on the time, aren't you? It's getting late."

"Yeah, I know."

"And after you put the dinosaur in the garage, you'll feed the hippos, right?"

"Yeah, yeah."

Angel resisted the urge to hit him. "I have to go now or I'll miss the bus." She picked up her books.

Sean nodded. "Yeah, Angel. Sure."

"Earth calling Android Boy," she shouted. "Your sister is leaving now. Say good-bye."

"Bye," Sean said.

By the time she was hurrying down the front stoop, Angel had already forgotten about Sean and whether or not he was going to remember his lunch or even remember to go to school. All she could think of was the day ahead of her: another day of misery at Midville High. Angel sighed. It wasn't even that they seemed hostile to her anymore. The only person who showed any real hostility was Suze Adams, and even Angel couldn't blame her for that. Once or twice Angel had started to go over to Suze, to try to make up for cutting her dead that time, but Suze had pointedly turned away. Everyone else was just indifferent. *It's probably just as well Suze hates me*, Angel decided as she charged toward the road. *If she came by now, B.J. would hang around the whole time. "Make yourself at home, Suze," I'd have to tell her. "But be careful not to sit on the ghost."*

Halfway across the lawn, she noticed a small, short-haired, black-and-brown dog with folded-over ears running in front of her. The dog was wearing a familiar paisley scarf around it neck.

Sparky! Sparky wearing one of her best scarves. Where Sparky was, B.J. was. She spun around.

B.J. was loping toward her across the grass. She had never seen him outside of the house before, lighted by the sun, a breeze from the Sound ruffling his hair. She was so surprised, she couldn't speak. He looked younger, somehow. Younger, and very real. That was it. He looked like a real boy, striding across the yard in the morning sunshine, his collar up and his hands jammed in his pockets. Like a boy who might walk beside you on the street, talking about the game on Saturday; like a boy who might suddenly lean over and give you a kiss. The memory of that first afternoon in the attic, when B.J. had put his arms around her, engulfed her unexpectedly. That was how it had felt in his arms, like he was real.

"Mornin'." B.J. stopped a few feet away. "And how's my favorite cheerleader on this beautiful autumn day?"

Angel frowned. It wasn't like him to be so cheerful. Or so friendly. Nor was it like her. "And just where do you think you're going with that mutt?"

He grinned. "Sparky's just walkin' us to the bus stop. But I'm goin' with you."

It must be the shock of seeing him like this. She couldn't have heard him right. He couldn't have said that he was going with *her*. Going where? "What are you, insane? You can't come with me. I'm going to school."

He pretended to be shocked. "No kiddin'? You're goin' t'school? And here I thought you were on your way to a big dance."

"Oh, very funny."

134

B.J. winked. "I'd offer to carry your books, bein' a gentleman, but it might look a little strange."

A little strange? "You are insane," she said quietly. "Completely and totally insane." Angel shifted her backpack. "But you are going nowhere with me."

"Yes, I am. I'm goin' to school."

"No, you are not."

"Oh, yes I are. We're ridin' on the bus together, and we're goin' to classes together." His smile looked younger, too. Softer. "I don't eat much lunch anymore, but I'm willin' t'watch you—"

Riding on the bus together, going to classes together. No wonder he looked cheerful . . . he'd come up with the ultimate torture for her. The two things she hated most in the universe, Midville High and B.J. Spatano, together at last.

"You are not coming with me," she repeated, "and that's final." Forgetting, she went to shove him away, and almost fell as her arm slid through him.

"Whoa, sweetheart," he laughed. He pushed against her to straighten her up. The leather of his jacket grazed her cheek. "Yes, I am coming," he whispered to the top of her head.

"No!" she pulled back, stamping her foot. "I'm sure you never bothered going to school when you were alive. Why break a perfect attendance record after all these years?"

He pulled one of her long, dark hairs from his jacket. "Let's just say I thought it might be fun."

"Well, it's not fun," said Angel, sounding more angry than she'd intended. "It's not fun, it's awful, and you're not going." She started to march away.

"You can't stop me," said B.J., his mouth almost pressed to her ear. "How are you going to stop me, Angel?"

Now, that was a good question. She walked faster. "What if someone sees you, you bonehead? Then what?"

He walked faster, too. "I told you before. No one can see me if I don't want them to."

"Except Sean."

"Except Sean." He picked a leaf from her shoulder. "He's a sensitive kid. But don't worry, princess, most people aren't sensitive. Most people are like you."

"Aren't you forgetting something?" She turned her sweetest smile on him. "I can see you, too."

"That's just because you're so stubborn," said B.J. "You don't even know what you can't do."

She sped up. No, this was not going to happen. How could she spend a whole day in the company of someone who made her want to scream after she'd been with him for only two minutes? She stopped suddenly, swinging around to face him. "Why can't you just leave me alone?" she demanded. "You are not coming, do you hear me?" She was shrieking. "I don't know why you've decided to persecute me like this, but I won't allow it!" She knew she was shrieking but she didn't care. "No! No! No! I will not let you come with me. You may be dead, you bum, but you're not deaf, are you?"

B.J. raised one eyebrow and nodded across the road. "Neither is Mrs. Morgen."

Angel blinked. "What?"

He nodded again. "Mrs. Morgen isn't deaf, either."

Very, very slowly, Angel turned to look behind her. Directly across the street was Mrs. Morgen, standing in the middle of her yard in her robe and slippers, arrested in the act of picking up the morning paper from the lawn. She was staring at Angel.

Angel smiled.

Mrs. Morgen, normally a chatty, even an overly chatty woman, didn't return the smile. She had the oddest expression on her face, as though she'd just seen a two-headed monster that was bleeding and couldn't decide whether to run away or rush to it with a Band-Aid.

Angel waved.

Mrs. Morgen, normally as friendly as a cocker spaniel, didn't return the wave.

"What's wrong with her?" whispered Angel. "She looked like she's seen a ghost."

B.J. started snickering. "I think it's more like she *hasn't* seen a ghost."

Hasn't seen a ghost! Angel's temperature rose about a hundred degrees. How long had Mrs. Morgen been standing there in her luminescent blue bathrobe and her fuzzy green slippers? Long enough to think that Angel had been screaming at a tree! Long enough to have heard Angel Lister tell a tree that it wasn't going to school with her.

"Are you all right, dear?" called Mrs. Morgen.

Angel nodded fervently. "Oh, yes, yes," she stammered. "Yes, Mrs. Morgen, I'm fine . . . I just . . . I . . ." she pointed behind her. "I was just rehearsing for the school play. The tryouts are this afternoon."

Mrs. Morgen didn't disguise her relief. "Oh, the school play," she said, smiling and nodding. "I see . . . you were rehearsing for the school play. Well, isn't that nice." She smiled and nodded some more. "For a minute there I almost thought . . ." Mrs. Morgen trailed off, laughing. "Well, good luck, dear. I hope you get the part." She tucked her paper under her arm. "What play did you say it was?"

B.J. rested a hand on Angel's shoulder. *"Topper,"* he suggested. "That was always one of my favorite shows. I loved the dog."

Oh, how she would have liked to hit him. Hard. "You probably never heard of it, Mrs. Morgen," she told her, smiling sweetly and moving away from that hand. "It's called *The Death of James Dean.*"

He'd stayed in the house for over three decades. Once in a while, he'd walked around the yard or taken Sparky for a run on the beach, but he'd never gone far. That was his first rule: Never leave the block. And then Angel Lister had moved in, and she'd made him so nuts that the next thing he knew, he was riding on the school bus, walking down the corridors of Midville High, sitting in classes, out in the world.

Well, rules were made to be broken, B.J. told himself as he sauntered down the hallway behind Angel. "Yo, princess," he called. "What class did you say we're goin' to next?"

She raised her head a little higher and started walking faster. She'd ignored him on the ride to school. She'd ignored him as they crossed the campus. She'd ignored him when they got inside.

And she was ignoring him still. Here he was, doing things he hadn't done in decades, just for her, because she made him so nuts that sometimes he wanted to give her one in the kisser and other times he almost felt sorry for her. And she wouldn't even speak to him! *Rules aren't the only things made to be broken,* thought B.J. as he followed her into a classroom. This was one of those times when he felt like he'd like to break *her*.

Angel rushed to her seat at the back of the room, leaving B.J. standing by himself at the door. He looked around. It was a math class. There was no mistaking it for anything else. The blackboard was covered with half-erased numbers, and everyone was huddled in groups, comparing their homework. Everyone, that is, except Angel. B.J. glanced worriedly in her direction and then went to find a place to sit.

He'd thought Angel was being her usual melodramatic self when she'd said that school was awful. Angel thought not having her own phone was awful. Angel thought getting a pimple was the end of the world. But only a few hours here with her had shown him that she wasn't exaggerating at all. It *was* awful.

B.J. made himself comfortable on the wide window ledge. School was awful because of Angel. She had no friends, she talked to no one, she never even raised her hand. At home she acted like the queen of the castle; here she acted like the kitchen maid—the kitchen maid with a chip on her shoulder. He stretched his legs out. He'd be having a good time if it weren't for her.

The bell rang, the door shut, the students took their seats; the teacher began to drone on. B.J. looked out the window.

It wasn't so bad being out in the world again. It was weird, but it wasn't so bad. It wasn't easy getting used to how much Midville had changed. The empty lots where they'd used to play had disappeared; the few houses he still recognized looked different; there was not one face he saw that he knew. But everything else had changed, too . . . the kids, the cars, the clothes, motorcycle technology. It was kind of exciting. He couldn't decide which knocked him out more, the chicks or the bikes.

And it was strange being back in school after all these years. Strange, but kind of pleasant. Everything was different here, too, but at the same time it wasn't really different. Different building, different kids, different teachers, different books— but the same feelings, the same him. Memories of the past returned so strongly that B.J. could almost believe he'd never left. When he followed Angel down the hall, he half-expected Mike Maris and Tony King to come around the corner, bent double with laughter. Half-expected Sunny Gibson in a straight, tight skirt and a sweater that buttoned up the back to swish into the hallway, smiling at him in that way she used to smile. Waited for Mr. Alsop to step out of his office, jerk his head, and say, "Spatano, I want to have a word with you. Now."

Angel was wrong about him. B.J. had always come to school when he was alive. Every day—rain, snow, or shine. On the whole, he'd liked school. He'd had friends here and things he liked to do.

He'd been a good student when he'd wanted to be.

But the best thing about school had been that it wasn't home. Home was where the hate was. At home he was nobody, nothing. At school he was someone else, someone hip and tough and cool. Someone who made people laugh, not yell at him and push him around. Sure, he'd gotten into trouble at school. He'd gotten into trouble for doing what he wasn't supposed to be doing, or not doing what he was supposed to be doing. But it wasn't like at home. At home he'd gotten into trouble just for being there; just for having his mother's smile.

B.J. watched a girls' gym class trot out to the hockey field. The girls were talking and walking close to each other, just the way he remembered they did.

But school wasn't like that for Angel. Angel didn't escape from home to school the way he had. Angel went to school like other people went to prison. Reluctantly, and with a negative attitude. He could tell from the way she watched the other kids that she didn't know who she was at school. She marched stiffly through the halls, her head held high, her mouth set, her eyes cold. *She might as well be wearing a sign that says, I DO NOT BELONG!*, thought B.J. *She might as well be wearing a sign that says, AND I DON'T WANT TO, SO THERE!*

Mrs. Wing's voice began to sound like a bass drum. B.J. watched the girls on the field hunch over their sticks, one of two of them shielding their eyes from the sun. So he knew that he was right about why she could see him. She wasn't just stuck-up, spoiled, selfish, and mean—she was lonely, too. Lonely and scared. He folded his arms across his chest. *Maybe Sean was right. Maybe Angel was almost human, after all.*

"Hey!" called B.J. "Where's the fire? Slow down. I wanna see the sights."

Angel didn't slow down. If she walked any faster, she'd be running. It had taken her the time that it took to walk from 52 Bluff Drive to the bus stop to realize that the only way to survive a day with William J. Spatano was to keep him as far away as possible. She'd been lucky so far. The bus had been so crowded that he'd had to stand in the aisle. He'd had to sit on the floor by the door in English, in the corner by the specimen jars in science, and on the window ledge in math, where he'd quickly fallen asleep. The most difficult time was while going from one class to another, like now, because he was always right there, either next to her or behind, talking and talking, blah, blah, blah.

There was a long, low whistle behind her. Angel glowered. *No prizes for guessing who that was*, she told herself. She glanced up in time to see a red-haired girl wearing tight purple jeans and a skimpy Lycra top swoosh by. Over her shoulder, she gave him a dirty look. That was the sort of sight B.J. Spatano was interested in!

"Man," B.J. said, sounding as happy as Lindy when her mother let her use her charge card. "Man, just look at these chicks. I'm really glad I came along. Things sure have improved since my day."

"It's too bad *you* haven't," Angel muttered.

He slipped his arm through hers. "So, now where, sweetheart? Time to feed yet?"

She looked down, so no one passing would see her lips moving. "No," she whispered, "history."

Her least-favorite class. Silvia and May were in history with her, sitting on the other side of the room, not even noticing her existence. Suze was in history with her, sitting at the back, pretending not to notice her existence. And Ms. Michaels was teaching history, standing right in front of Angel, noticing her only too well. Ms. Michaels hated Angel. Ms. Michaels hated Angel because, worried that Ms. Michaels wouldn't understand how different Angel's courses in Maryland had been, Angel had tried to explain how things were done in Lisson Park. Ms. Michaels had misunderstood. She'd seemed to think Angel was criticizing her ability. "If you want things done the way they are in Lisson Park, Ms. Lister," Ms. Michaels had informed her, much to the adolescent amusement of the rest of the class, "then I suggest you go back there. I certainly don't need you to tell me how to teach." Since then, Ms. Michaels had never let an opportunity go by to treat Angel with sarcasm and scorn.

"What?" He pressed closer. "Speak up, doll. I can't hear you, there's too much noise." He squeezed her arm. "Everybody's havin' such a good time."

Not everybody. *Doll.* She'd like to *doll* him. "History!" she hissed. Louder than she'd intended.

The two girls ahead of her turned around.

Angel glared back.

"Great," B.J. said. "I always liked history."

Angel groaned inwardly. *Oh, sure he liked history. The history of the internal combustion engine.* She covered her mouth with her hand. "Look," she

143

whispered, "why don't you just go smoke in the boys' room or something for this period?"

B.J. grinned. "What are y'tryin' t'do? Bring back my lost youth?"

"No." Angel turned the corner sharply. "I thought that was what you were trying to do when you fell asleep during the lecture on real numbers."

"I said I liked history," B.J. repeated as Angel pushed open a classroom door. "But I never dug math. It lacks personal warmth." He winked. "Sort of like you."

Angel slipped into her seat at the front. She expected him to sit on the window ledge or in a corner, but instead, somehow knowing no one sat there, he slid into the desk behind her. He stretched his legs under her chair, giving her a kick. She kicked back.

Ms. Michaels, going through something on her desk, looked up and made one of her dead-fish faces in Angel's direction. Angel turned away. She took out her notebook.

B.J. kicked her chair again. "Man," he said, "I really do love the way these ladies dress. And the way they look. And the way they smell."

He was chewing gum. She was sure he was chewing gum. She snapped open her notes.

He grabbed her shoulder. "Hey," he practically whistled. "There's Suze Adams. I didn't know she was in this class."

Angel shook him off, concentrating on finding her place. *Suze must be out sick sometime. Why not today?*

B.J. grabbed her again. "Angel, that's her, isn't

it? With the squashy mouth? You couldn't forget that mouth."

"I could," she mumbled.

He leaned closer. He *was* chewing gum. "What?"

It hadn't occurred to her before that B.J.'s fascination with Suze was personal. Not personal like a real boy's. Somehow, this idea annoyed her even more. Surely Suze wasn't B.J.'s type. If he were a real boy, he'd go for girls with beehive hairdos and bubblegum-pink lipstick and tight, straight skirts.

"She got a boyfriend?" he persisted.

Apparently Suze Adams, with her pouty mouth and her boy's haircut, *was* William J. Spatano's type. Angel jerked her chair forward.

"How do I know if she has a boyfriend?" she hissed back. "All I know is that she thinks she's something."

B.J.'s lips touched Angel's ear. "She *is* something."

She could scream. First she wanted to slug him, and then she wanted to scream: *You spamhead! What is your problem? You're dead. You can't talk about girls like that.*

Ms. Michaels stood up. Around Angel, conversations trailed off as chairs were scraped into place and all eyes faced the front of the room. All eyes but Angel's. Angel was doodling violently on the cover of her notebook, still silently arguing with B.J. *And even if you weren't dead, you're such a complete loser that no girl who wasn't desperate would even nod to you in the hall.*

Ms. Michaels asked for attention. Everyone but Angel gave it to her. *Why don't you just crawl back*

145

in your grave and leave me alone? Why don't you go haunt Suze Adams if you think she's so great?

"Today, we're going to be discussing the 'specter that haunted Europe'," Ms. Michaels announced.

The specter that haunted Europe, Angel repeated to herself. *Yeah, tell me about it.*

The class went hysterical.

Angel, disturbed from her own thoughts by the shrieks and laughter, looked up. Everyone was watching her. Why was everybody watching her? Benjy Hayman, the cretin on her right, was practically choking to death, and right behind her B.J. was kicking the floor, he was laughing so hard. *The specter that haunted Europe. Yeah, tell me about it.* Angel's eyes met Ms. Michaels'. That was when she knew. She hadn't been thinking silently. She had said it out loud. "The specter that haunted Europe," she'd said. "Yeah, tell me about it." And Ms. Michaels thought she'd been talking to *her*.

Ms. Michaels smiled, with an effect as warm as having a wet rag thrown in your face. "You wouldn't happen to know what that phrase means, would you, Ms. Lister?" Her tone implied that she thought there was probably a better chance that Angel spoke Greek.

The laughter had settled, but everyone was still looking at her. Twenty-five people, not one of whom liked her, were waiting for Angel to speak. She cleared her throat.

B.J. leaned toward her. "War," he said.

Angel clenched her teeth. "Go away."

"What?" Ms. Michaels walked toward her. "Did you say something, Ms. Lister? Something you want to share with the class, so they'll know that you're not really as bad at history as you seem to be?"

"War," B.J. repeated. "Tell her it's war."

A trill of laughter ran through the room.

Angel stared into Ms. Michaels' round, gray eyes. "Um . . ."

"I'm tellin' you," said B.J., his cheek against hers, "the specter that haunted Europe was war."

"Well?" said Ms. Michaels. "We're all waiting."

"What are you, deaf?" B.J. shouted. He shoved her seat. "The specter that haunted Europe was war!"

"Shut up!" Angel ordered. "For two seconds, just shut your big mouth!"

The classroom froze. For one nanosecond, no one breathed and no one moved. And then that nanosecond passed. Everyone but Ms. Michaels started laughing at once.

"'Shut up'?" asked Ms. Michaels. "Did you say 'shut up'?"

Angel shook her head. "Oh, no," she said. "No, I didn't say shut up."

"Yes, you did," said Benjy Hayman. "I heard you. You said, 'Shut your big mouth.'"

Angel gaped at Ms. Michaels in horror. "But not to you," she tried to explain. "I wasn't telling *you* to shut your big mouth."

"Well, I'm certainly glad to hear that." Ms. Michaels put her hands on Angel's desk and leaned forward. "So whom were you talking to?"

From the back of the room a girl's voice whispered loudly, "Probably the specter that haunted Europe."

❦   ❦   ❦

"Detention!" Angel stormed down Bluff Drive and across the lawn of number 52. "I've never had to stay for detention before in my life!"

B.J. jogged behind her. He was beginning to change his mind slightly about modern fashion. There was a distinct advantage in chasing a girl who wore high heels over chasing a girl who wore running shoes. Angel had been moving like a torpedo since they'd gotten off the bus. "Don't lose your cool, Angel," he shouted. "You get used to it, believe me. It's no big deal."

"Shut up!" Angel put her hands to her ears. "I don't want to hear anymore!" she screamed. "Not one more word."

He reached for her as she ran up the path, but she slipped from his grasp. "For Pete's sake, Angel. What are y'blamin' me for? I'm the guy who was tryin' to help."

"Help?" She stopped on the stoop, shaking with fury. "Oh, right, big help you are. Making Ms. Michaels hate me even more than she already did. Mortifying me in front of the entire class. Do you have any idea who's in that class, you idiot?"

Now what was she talking about? "Yeah," he said, "I know. Suze Adams."

"No, not Suze Adams. Silvia Samson and May Lewis are in that class, that's who!"

Was that supposed to impress him? If she'd said Elvis and Little Richard, now, that really would be something. . . . "So who's Silvia whatshername and May Lewis?"

Angel sneered. His old man would've told her to be careful or her face would freeze that way.

148

"Only the two most popular cheerleaders in my year, that's who."

Cheerleaders. He tried to recall the faces in the room. "You don't mean the blondes with the home permanents, do you?"

If he were a plant and not a ghost, her look would have withered him.

"Those 'home permanents' only cost at least a hundred dollars apiece." She kicked the railing, shaking the porch. "You should've seen their faces when everyone was laughing at me. I could never get into their crowd now, even if I wanted to."

B.J. shrugged. "So what? Those girls aren't nothin' special. What do you care if you're in with them or not?"

"Oh, I'll be sure to take your advice," Angel said, speeding ahead again. "Especially since the only thing you've ever been in your life was probably jail." The door slammed in his face.

He'd seen her in bad moods. He'd seen her angry. He'd seen her touchy. He'd heard her scream. But he'd never seen her this mad before. If he were alive, she really might have killed him.

But he wasn't going to let that stop him from making her see reason. He'd been right to go to school with her. Seeing her in school, he'd seen her loneliness wrapped around her like a suit of armor. No wonder she was so angry all the time. No wonder she was always crying. She was miserable. For the first time it had really hit him how hard the move must have been for Angel. She hadn't just left her school and her friends, she'd left her father and her life as well. Not that that didn't mean she wasn't her own worst enemy. She was that. As usual, she didn't give an inch. He followed her into the house.

"But it wasn't my fault," he said as he came through the door. "Even you hafta admit that. It was your fault. If you'd listened t'me—"

"Listened to you!" Now she was shrieking. "You spent the entire morning ogling girls and falling asleep. How was I supposed to know you really knew something about history? I didn't even know you could read!"

"Because I told you I liked history, that's how. It was my best subject—"

She started running up the stairs. "No!" she shouted. "No more."

He stared at her furious and disappearing back. So he'd been wrong. He couldn't handle Angel Lister. P. T. Barnum couldn't have handled Angel Lister. P. T. Barnum, the U.S. Marines, and that guy from that Shakespeare play about the shrew, whatever his name was—all of them together couldn't have handled Angel. Because she would never admit she was wrong. She would never ask for help. *Brother!* B.J. jammed his hands in his pockets. If she wasn't the most infuriating person he'd ever known, he'd like to know who was. He shouldn't even waste his time worrying about her.

Sean came out of the kitchen with a peanut butter sandwich in his hand. He looked from the stairway to B.J. "Bad day?"

B.J. gazed at the ceiling as the attic door slammed shut. "There've been better." He shouldn't waste his time worrying about her, but somehow he couldn't help it.

Chapter 9
You Never Can Tell

The class was in chaos. The girls were wiping the tears and smudged makeup from their faces. The boys were banging on the desks and slapping each other. Ms. Michaels was laughing so hard she had to take off her glasses and rub her eyes. People must have laughed this much before in the history of the world, but Angel hadn't been present then. And she hadn't been the cause. "Maybe they're all crazy in Lisson Park," someone shouted out from the back of the room. "Maybe that's why she's so strange."

Angel sat in her seat, staring over Ms. Michaels' head, rigid as steel.

Ms. Michaels recovered first. "I hope you realize that you'll never make any friends at Midville High now, Ms. Lister," Ms. Michaels informed her. She snapped her glasses back in place. "Not now that everyone knows exactly what kind of person you are." She did her impersonation of a disapproving trout. "The kind who tells her teacher to shut up! The kind who doesn't even know what the specter that haunted Europe was!"

There was a rumble of agreement. Voices exploded like gun shots.

"That's right!"

"I bet she doesn't even have a phone in her room!"

"Phone? She probably has to share the bathroom!"

"She probably doesn't own a microwave!"

Benjy Hayman leaned across the aisle and leered at her. "Tell the truth, Angel," he wheedled. "Isn't your mother that waitress who drives the blue van?"

"What's her name?" someone else asked. "Hamburger Hannah?"

"Is that where you learned to tell your teachers to shut up?" Ms. Michaels smiled conspiratorially at the rest of the class. "In a diner?"

"You don't understand!" Angel screamed. "You don't understand! I wasn't talking to you, Ms. Michaels. I swear I wasn't. I'm really very nice." She turned in her chair. "I used to have my own phone," she explained to the class. "I really did. I had a pink phone with a private line."

Silvia Samson tossed her curls. "In your dreams," she hooted.

May Lewis sputtered in giggles. "Where did you say you sleep, Angel?" she called. "In the attic?! In the attic with the maid?"

"No," Silvia squealed. "In the attic with the pink phone!"

Ms. Michaels leaned on Angel's desk. "Is that how you do it in Lisson Park?" she demanded. "You sleep in the attic, and you don't pay attention in class? Is that how it's done?"

Angel looked from one face to another. "No! No! that's not how we do it. Everything's perfect in Lisson Park! Absolutely perfect."

"It is!" shrieked someone else. "It is how they do it! They sleep in the attic and tell their teachers to shut up!"

152

"I don't believe this!" wailed Angel. "It's all B.J.'s fault. Why doesn't anyone yell at him?"

Angel woke up to the sound of rain. The blankets were tangled around her feet, and her face was damp with sweat. *Perfect,* she was thinking as her eyes slowly opened. *Lisson Park is perfect. . . .* Bouncy music and shrill voices drifted up from the living room. Sean must be watching the Saturday cartoons. With a certain amount of relief, she dragged herself from her dream and rolled over with a heavy sigh. *What a nightmare!* She cringed at the thought of it. *What a horrible, terrible nightmare!* She was more exhausted now than she had been when she'd finally fallen asleep last night. "At least there's one consolation," Angel said to the ceiling. "At least my bad dreams are still worse than my life." She pushed aside the covers. "If only barely."

How could nothing really awful happen to you for sixteen whole years and then everything go wrong at once? Angel wondered. She stared at herself in the bathroom mirror. She saw the same pretty face that had always looked back at her. Only now it wasn't the face of the most popular girl in school, it was the face of a loser. Angel picked up her washcloth. By Monday she'd be the laughingstock of the whole school. Even the janitor would have heard what a fool she'd made of herself yesterday. What Ms. Michaels had said in her dream was true. She never would make any friends in Midville now. She wasn't just a loser, she was the loser of the millennium. Once she'd had everything, and now what did she have? Angel answered her own question. "Nothing," she said out loud. She threw the cloth at the mirror.

"Nothing at all."

She opened the door of her room. *No, not nothing,* she thought, seeing a pair of feet in dirty black boots resting on her desk. *I still have one thing. It just isn't something I want.*

The one thing Angel did have was sprawled in her armchair, waiting for her with a thoughtful expression on his face. He'd kept away from her after they got back, which wasn't too hard, since she wouldn't come out of her room. But he'd heard sobbing over his head long after Denise and Sean had gone to sleep, and he'd remembered the other unhappy teenager who had lived in that room. *I'm gonna talk to her again,* he'd decided somewhere around dawn. *She needs a friend, and I'm gonna be it whether she likes it or not.*

She wasn't going to like it. He could tell that by the way she didn't exactly look at him as she came into the room. "What are *you* doing here?" she asked sourly.

Start slow, B.J. warned himself. He swung his legs to the floor. "I just wanted t'say that I'm genuinely sorry for what happened yesterday." He stood up, his hand on his heart. "Not that I think I'm completely t'blame, you understand. I don't really see how I'm t'blame at all, if you want the truth. But I *am* sorry."

She strode past him. "Get lost."

"I see suffering's not exactly makin' you a better person, is it?" He followed her across the room. Maybe there wasn't any point in going too slow. "Y'know," he said, rushing in, "I've been givin' this

154

a lot of thought, princess, and you're gonna hafta change your attitude, or you really won't have any friends. Maybe if you could laugh at yourself a little—"

She wasn't even smiling now.

"I don't have to laugh at myself," Angel snapped, her eyes firmly fixed on the mirror over her bureau. "Thanks to you, everybody else does it for me."

"Aw, come on . . . y'hafta admit, it was pretty funny." He touched her shoulder. "And anyway, they weren't laughin' at you, Angel. They were laughin' with you."

She picked up her brush as though she might hit him with it. "Silvia Samson and May Lewis were not laughing with me."

He removed his hand. "You kill me, you know that? You really kill me."

"I should be so lucky," Angel said. There was no more than an inch or two between them, but the reflection showed only her bed, her desk, her chair, the poster of her favorite group hanging on the wall, and Angel herself. She glared at him in the mirror anyway.

He leaned closer. "I'm tellin' you, sweetheart, you better start listenin' to some advice."

She ripped the brush through her hair. "I don't take advice from a person who thinks that 'Hound Dog' is one of the most important songs ever written," she informed him coolly.

"Well you oughta," he said with conviction. "Y' never can tell, you know, Angel. You've gotta give people a chance. But do you? No. You don't talk to anyone in your classes. You don't say hello to anyone in the hall. You don't smile." He moved so he was looking into her face. She refused to meet his eyes. "And how come you don't go to the cafeteria? How come you sit by yourself in some empty science room?"

"I told you yesterday. It's too noisy in the cafeteria. I need the time for homework. I have a lot of other things to do when I get home, you know."

If she didn't slow down on the brushing she was going to be bald. "Oh, come on, princess. Nobody would rather eat by themselves in a room surrounded by dead things in jars when they could be in a nice cafeteria with a whole bunch of people talkin' and laughin'."

She threw the brush at the wall. "Well that just shows how much you know, doesn't it? Just because you wanted to sit around gawking at Suze Adams all through lunch doesn't mean I did."

She really was too much. If it wasn't one thing, it was another. "I didn't wanna sit around gawking at Suze Adams," he mimicked. Bending down, he picked the brush off the floor and put it carefully on the dresser. "We're not talkin' about Suze, Angel. We're talkin' about you. You can't hole up like you're doin'. You're your own worst enemy—"

"Oh, please," she begged, rolling her eyes. "Spare me the clichés."

"It's not a cliché. It's true. You don't do yourself any favors, sweetheart, struttin' around with your nose in the air, keepin' yourself apart. If nobody's friendly to you, it's because they think you're stuck-up, like those cheerleader geeks you're so worried about."

156

"Geeks!" She was willing to meet his eyes now. "You, William Spatano, the missing link between pond scum and the toad, are calling Silvia Samson and May Lewis geeks?"

She turned to storm off, but he grabbed her by the shoulder, holding her hard. "Look," he said, his voice more gentle than his hands, "I know you don't wanna hear this, but—"

"At last you're right about something. *I don't wanna hear this.*"

"I've really been thinkin' about you a lot, and I understand what you're going through. I mean, there's stuff I've never told anyone . . . you know, about my folks and my bro—stuff like that, and . . . well, it's just that I know what it feels like."

"You are not here," she said flatly. "You have been history for over thirty years, and I do not have to listen to a single stupid word you say."

He tightened his hold. "Oh, yes, you do. You can't go on livin' in the past, Angel. Lisson Park's gone. Forget about it. Start something new, something better." He turned her to face him. "You better cut this crap, princess. You're not the only person in the world that's ever been scared, you know. You're not the only person who couldn't have what they wanted."

Her expression described scorn. "Try to concentrate on what I'm saying," she ordered. "I do not like you. There is nothing you could say that would interest me one infinitesimal, microscopic, teensy-weensy bit, unless it's good-bye."

Why did he bother? Why waste his breath? *Well, what'd you expect?* B.J. asked himself. *Thanks?* He

157

took his hands away, holding them in the air as though someone were pointing a gun at him. "Don't talk t'me like that, Angel. You know I hate it when you give me that princess spiel of yours."

Melodramatic as ever, she pointed toward the door. "Why don't you just go to hell, where you belong?"

"I don't hafta," B.J. said, walking backwards through the closed door. "Livin' with you is hell enough."

Angel leaned against the refrigerator, reading the note Denise had left her. *Feed your brother, do the laundry, straighten up the kitchen, make sure Sean cleans Germy's cage, take Sean to the mall on the bus and buy him a new pair of sneakers, bring back change.*

Has anyone ever been as unappreciated or put-upon as I am? Angel wondered. For just an instant, the image of B.J. saying, "I understand . . . there's stuff I never told anyone . . . ," came into her mind, but she shoved it away. She wasn't going to start worrying about the problems of some dead hood. She had enough problems of her own.

Scowling, Angel looked at the lined yellow paper. It was a punishment, that was what it was. Denise was punishing her for not fixing Sean his supper last night. She was making her pay for refusing to come out of her room. She threw the note on the counter and looked out at the rain. Of course, it wouldn't be a pleasant, sunny day. Of course, it would be pouring. It was a miracle it wasn't snowing or something. What, no tornado? No typhoon? Wasn't it about time

Long Island had an earthquake? She sighed wearily. All the way to the mall on public transportation with Baby Weirdo. She'd better make sure they got back before dark, or the bus might turn back into a pumpkin pulled by six white mice. The distinct smell of scorching toast broke into her thoughts.

"Mom said I can pick," Sean said, as Angel set two golden squares of toast in front of him. "She said I can have any sneaker I want as long as it doesn't cost too much." He lifted the bread and peered underneath. "She said not to let you talk me out of anything I really wanted."

It wasn't enough that her mother treated her like a servant. She treated her like a servant who couldn't be trusted. "What are you doing?" Angel demanded. "Don't play with it, just eat it."

"I'm not playing with it. I was looking to see if it was burnt or not." He flipped over the toast, charred side up, and made a face. "I don't understand how you only burn it on one side all the time," he said. "Do you do it on purpose, or what?"

"Charcoal's good for your lungs," Angel answered. "And, besides, it's not my fault, and you know it. It's that stupid toaster." She heaped grape jelly on her own incinerated slice. Her mother spent a fortune on equipment to prepare hamburgers and fried-egg sandwiches for construction workers but expected her own children to use a broken toaster. "She'll be sorry when it blows up in my face."

Sean reached for the peanut butter. "Why don't you ask B.J. to fix it?"

The jelly turned to lemon in Angel's mouth. "B.J.?"

"Yeah, sure." He nodded. "He's always fixin' things around here. That leak in the bathroom, Mom's typewriter . . ." He bit into his toast, peanut butter squishing out of the corners of his mouth. "B.J. fixes the van all the time. That's why I convinced Mom to keep it at the back, so he can work on it at night without anyone seeing anything strange."

"B.J.? B.J. Spatano is our handyman?"

Sean wiped his mouth with his sleeve. "I wouldn't let him hear you call him that. He does it because he feels bad for Mom."

"The golden-hearted hood," Angel said. "Spare me."

"But it's true. He even fixed the washing machine. Remember the time it flooded the cellar? Well, it was B.J. who got it working again."

Angel pushed her plate away. It was difficult to decide what made her madder, that B.J. should have the nerve to do things for them out of pity or that they clearly needed him to. "I'd rather eat ashes than ask him for help."

"You *are* eating ashes," Sean said, looking from her to his breakfast. "And, anyway, I don't see why you say that. B.J.'s cool."

She made a face. "Only in the sense that he's dead."

Sean lowered his voice. "You should be nicer to him, Angel. I don't think B.J. had a very happy life."

Angel stared at him. *What was this? Be nice to B.J. Spatano day? Feel sorry for B.J. Spatano week? So what if he had had a bad time? He wasn't the only one.* "Then why doesn't he just crawl into his grave and get it over with, like everybody else does?"

160

Sean's expression became almost solemn. He leaned toward her. "But B.J. doesn't have a grave," he whispered. "He's an unquiet soul."

"You mean he's got a big mouth," she said, getting up and beginning to clear the table.

But Sean was completely serious. "No, really, Angel. You don't know anything."

"I'm not the only one." She put the dishes in the sink.

"But, Angel, he was only nineteen. Don't you think that's sad? He was just a kid, and this enormous truck jackknifed across the highway and killed him." Sean's voice became even lower, barely louder than breathing. "There was this big explosion and fire and everything. . . . There wasn't anything left."

Angel dumped the burnt toast into the garbage. There was more than enough of B.J. Spatano left to suit her. "Is that what he told you?" she asked over her shoulder. "That he's an unquiet soul without a grave?"

Sean shook his head. "No, that's what Mr. Stucker told me."

She put her hands on her hips. "And what did B.J. say? Did he tell you that he killed someone? Did he tell you how he died escaping from the scene of a crime?"

"He told me I remind him a little of his brother."

"That's it?"

Sean looked down, scraping up some spilled peanut butter with his finger. "He doesn't ever talk about it."

She put the milk and juice back in the refrigerator

and shut the door hard. "It's the only thing I don't blame him for," Angel said.

If anyone had asked Angel earlier that morning what could possibly be worse than riding on a bus, in the rain, with her brother, to go to the mall and buy *him* a pair of sneakers and nothing for herself, she would have said, "Nothing." Just being seen in public with Sean was enough to ruin anybody's day.

But she would have been wrong.

Angel sat in the aisle seat, watching the buildings speed by through the opposite window. There was one thing worse than taking public transportation with Android Boy in a minor deluge, and that one thing worse was sitting behind them, resting his chin on the back of their seat, staring out the window as Sean pointed out the sights. She wasn't sure whose bright idea it was to bring B.J. along, but not five minutes after the bus pulled out, B.J. leaned his head between hers and Sean's and said, "You got any gum? Buses always make me kinda seasick."

"There's a Taco Bell," Sean was saying. "That's Mexican food."

"That's amazing," said B.J. "Mexican food on Long Island."

"And look, over there's a Dunkin' Donuts."

Angel was pretending that she wasn't with him. Let the rest of the bus think he was crazy, talking to himself: she couldn't care less. Glancing over, she noticed how close B.J.'s head was to Sean's, the easy way he had one hand on the little boy's shoulder. *I guess he must have had a younger brother,* she found

162

herself thinking. And then wondered why she'd thought that. Who cared about B.J. Spatano's brother?

"Hey, look!" Sean suddenly bellowed, scrambling to his knees in his seat, the seat he was sharing with his sister. "Look! Those guys have bikes like yours!"

Trying to ignore the fact that several heads had turned in their direction, Angel glanced over. The least she could do was make it appear that he was talking to her. Two helmeted figures sped past the bus in a spray of rainwater.

"Harleys," said B.J. dismissively.. But then he shook his head. "You wouldn't catch me out in this weather, though. I don't drive in storms."

Angel folded her arms across her chest. "It's too bad you don't feel the same way about riding in buses," she whispered.

"Now, remember," Angel instructed Sean as they entered the Midville Plaza, "if that hood causes any trouble, any at all, you're the one who's going to hang."

"Don't worry," Sean said. "I told you, he's cool."

B.J. winked at her. "Like ice."

"Give me a break," Angel snapped.

Up until today, Angel had always had a weak spot for malls. She and Lindy had spent some of the best years of their lives in the mall back home. She'd never had to bring back change then.

But being in a mall with Lindy Porterfield and being in a mall with B.J. Spatano were not the same thing. Even if she'd had any money to spend on herself, she would have loathed every second.

163

B.J. had to check everything out. The plants, the stores, the waterfall, the groups of kids hanging out on benches. He loved the electronic map. "Man, this is really hot." He had to be dragged out of the music store. *"This* is an LP?" he kept saying, staring at the CDs. "Geez, I wonder if Mike and Tony know." Unless watched every second, he wandered off to check out toy stores or to trail after girls.

Angel squeezed Sean's arm. "You'd better keep an eye on him, Sean Lister," she threatened. "I mean it. Or the Lone Ranger here is going to have a little ghostly Tonto to keep him company for eternity."

"Hey, look there," B.J. cried. "It's a McDonald's, and it ain't a drive-in. It's got tables and everything. I wouldn't mind seein' what it's like inside."

"Mom won't let us go in McDonald's," said Sean. Angel kept walking.

"How come? I always thought McDonald's was okay."

"Because of Elvis," said Sean.

Angel couldn't help herself. She stopped and turned around. "What are you talking about now, you dweeble?"

"It's true," Sean whined.

"Elvis?" B.J. repeated. "Elvis works in McDonald's?"

That did it. "Just shut up, both of you," she whispered, "or we're going home."

But no one was listening to her except a middle-aged woman sitting on a bench with her shopping bag. She gave Angel a curious look.

"No," Sean was saying. "It's because he ate so many hamburgers that he died."

"What?" B.J. asked, gazing at him in horror. "Are you tellin' me that Elvis is dead?"

Angel turned on her heel. "I'm surprised you don't know him," she snapped.

B.J. disappeared somewhere between the escalator and Neat Feet, their destination. As far as Angel was concerned, it was the first positive thing that had happened all day.

"Let's just leave him," she suggested. "It's too bad if he can't find his way home."

"I bet I know where he is," Sean said.

"Let's hope not," said Angel.

B.J. was in Electroland. "I told you he loves my Nintendo," said Sean. There was a crowd gathered round KungFu Kowboy, watching in amazement as the machine played itself. "He's pretty good," Sean said.

"Well, that's a relief," said Angel.

Why did everything happen to her? She stared nervously through the gaping onlookers, trying to find a way of catching B.J.'s attention. *Who are you kidding?* she asked herself. *You have to turn the TV off to get either of them even to look at you when there's a ballgame on. There's no way he's going to look up from that.*

Sean glanced over at her. "You want me to get him?"

Angel took a deep breath. "No," she said, raising her head. "You've done enough."

She jostled through the crowd, trying to ignore the fact that everyone was looking at her. *Pow! Wop! Whizz! Blipblipblipblipbloop* went the machine. She stood behind B.J., pretending that she was staring at the screen, and said one simple word, calmly and clearly. "Now!"

"But I can't stop now, Angel," he answered. "I'm winnin' here."

"Now!

"Don't ever do that again," she hissed as he followed her out. "From now on, you stay with me."

He pulled her hair. "Like glue."

"Which do you think?" Sean held up a sneaker in each hand.

Angel's eyes were on B.J., picking through the work boots at the far end of the store. Some glue. "What does it matter?" she asked, not really paying much attention to him. "They're both exactly the same."

"No, they're not. One has orange-and-black laces, and the other has purple and red. And the soles are different colors."

Angel closed her eyes. It was too much, it really was. When she opened them again, Sean was trying on another pair, the ones with blue-and-silver laces and navy trim, and B.J. was facing toward her, grinning. She almost didn't recognize him. *What a gorgeous guy,* she caught herself thinking before she realized who it was. And then came her second realization. He wasn't looking at her. He was smiling over her head. Angel turned. There, halfway into the store, her arms filled with shopping bags and staring right at Angel, was Suze. She was wearing black leggings, a black turtleneck, and a black leather jacket painted with stars. It was not Angel's style, of course, but if the look on B.J.'s face was anything to

166

go by, it was pretty effective.

Angel acted as though she hadn't seen Suze. She grabbed Sean's foot and started examining it closely. "Is that comfortable?" she asked in a loud, bright voice. "Do you think there's enough room to grow?"

"Get off!" Sean shook her away. "Have house-wives taken over your body or something? What're you talking about, 'room to grow'?"

"On the other hand," she continued, "they do look easier to clean than—"

"Angel!"

Sean looked up. There was nothing she could do: she had to turn around. "Suze!"

"I tried to catch you after class yesterday," Suze said, apparently having forgotten that they weren't speaking, "but you disappeared so quickly, and I didn't see you at lunch. . . ."

"Me?"

Suze's head bobbed up and down. "Yeah, *you.*" She really did have a nice laugh. "I couldn't believe you told old flounder-face to shut up like that. Nobody could!"

Suze's eyes were wide with wonder—and something else, something Angel couldn't identify.

"That woman is such a pain. She's so mean and picky, and she never gives anybody a break. Damon Haller nearly got suspended from the basketball team because Ms. Michaels wouldn't give him just one more point on his midterm. One lousy point! Is that miserable, or what? And do you know what she did to me? She took ten points off my first essay because it wasn't 'formal' enough. *Formal!* 'It's not

167

a dress,' I felt like telling her. 'It's a five-page paper on the roots of modern Europe.'" She made a rueful face. "Of course, I didn't tell her that. I didn't tell her anything. But you! You stood up to her!"

My God, thought Angel. *It's admiration. Suze Adams likes me again!* She was grateful she was sitting down.

"I think it's disgusting the way she's always sniping at you," Suze was saying. "Everybody does."

Angel prayed her astonishment didn't show in her face. *Everybody? Who was everybody? Everybody but Silvia Samson and May Lewis, maybe.*

"She's just giving you a hard time because you're new."

Angel managed to speak at last. "Do you think so? You don't think it's just because she hates me?"

"Nah," said Suze. "Don't take it personally. Ms. Michaels hates everyone."

"Really?"

Suze sat down. "You haven't heard anything yet," she began.

By the time Suze had told her a few Ms. Michaels stories, Angel was wiping tears of laughter from her eyes. Maybe she wasn't such a loser, after all. Maybe things really weren't as bad as she'd thought.

"Didn't I tell you she was a neat chick?"

Angel jumped. B.J.! She'd been enjoying herself so much that she'd totally forgotten him and Sean. She looked around. Sean was sitting with a shoe box on his lap, rigid with boredom, and B.J. was sprawled on the other side of Suze, looking like he'd just won the lottery.

"Well, I'd better go now," Suze said, suddenly

getting to her feet. She nodded over her shoulder. "I left my sister by the sneakers."

Angel looked over to where a small, dark girl was sitting with her arms folded and a bored expression on her face. So she wasn't the only one who got stuck baby-sitting, either. She glanced at B.J. Had he looked after his little brother, too?

Suze picked up her bags. "Look, I know this is really late notice, Angel, but there's a party tonight—no big deal, just some friends, but it'd be great if you could come."

"I'd love to," said Angel, without even thinking, without even worrying about sounding too eager.

Suze smiled. "Excellent. Now get out a pen and write this down. . . ."

It wasn't until Suze had left the store that Angel realized she couldn't go to her party, after all.

"Why not?" asked Sean. "You have the address."

Angel gave him the look she usually reserved for insects that mistakenly wandered onto her picnic plate. "Yeah, Einstein, but I don't have anything to wear, do I?"

"What are y'talkin' about?" B.J. moved over to the seat Suze had vacated. "You have nothin' to wear? You have more clothes than Macy's."

"But nothing *new.*" She kept her eyes on her brother. "I can't go to my first party here in *old* clothes."

B.J. laid a hand on her shoulder. "Sweetheart, none of these people have ever seen your clothes before. They're not old t'them."

Angel smiled grimly at her brother. "I wouldn't

169

expect someone who wears the same disgusting clothes every day to understand about a thing like this."

B.J. gave her a squeeze. "Why don't you relax a little, Angel? You can bet your life Suze ain't buyin' nothin' to wear tonight."

How did he always know exactly the right thing to say to make her furious? Was it a natural talent, or could he read her mind? Whatever it was, it made her more determined than ever.

Angel grabbed Sean. "Sean," she said urgently and sincerely. "Sean, you have got to help me."

Sean tightened his grip on his shoe box. "No."

"Please, I'm begging you. I'm your only sister. And I'll pay you back. Just let me use your shoe money. Just this once, Sean. We'll come back next week and get your sneakers."

"But Mom—"

"Mom won't know. She's got a trillion other things to think about. Unless you remind her, she'll have forgotten all about your new sneakers by the time she gets home."

"But I want these. I—"

"You'll get them, Sean. You'll get them next week. Monday. I'll take the money out of my savings. We'll come after school on Monday." She could tell he was weakening.

"Promise?"

"Hope to die."

"Watch out what y'wish for," said B.J.

But Sean looked thoughtful. "What interest?"

"Ten percent."

"That's too low."

170

She *would* have the only kid brother in the world who thought about interest rates.

"Fifteen."

"Eighteen and a half."

"Done!" screamed Angel. "Wait right here," she ordered. She raced from the store.

Angel pulled on the third top, a black Lycra with a high neck but a low back, and stepped out of her cubicle to see how she looked in the full-length mirrors at the end of the dressing room.

She joined the girls frowning at their reflections as they twisted from side to side. She wasn't sure. She took a step forward. It wasn't really her style. The blue one had been more her style. Gavin would love the blue top. She stepped back. She moved to the left. She was sure Gavin wouldn't like this. Not on her. Gavin himself favored pastel colors and classic clothes. He didn't believe in standing out. "I don't want to look like a freak," Gavin always said. "I want to look like everybody else." When he said "I," he meant "we." She moved to the right. She didn't look like a freak, but she *did* look different. You couldn't wear this top and not be noticed. She turned to check the back.

"That's the one," said B.J. He was leaning in the doorway of an empty stall, watching her closely.

How long had he been there?

"The blue was too fussy."

Long enough. She glanced at the other girls. *Thank God*, she thought. *At least they're all covered.*

"And the green isn't really you." He winked.

She held her breath. If she held her breath, she

171

wouldn't start screaming in front of everybody. Slowly, she walked back to her stall.

B.J. followed. "But this one's cool," he was saying. "You look like a million."

"Oh, that's a real compliment, coming from you," she hissed. "What are you doing here? I thought I told you to stay with Sean."

"No, you didn't. You told me to stay with you."

She clenched her teeth. "But not in the dressing room, you pervert."

"Pervert? I'm not a pervert. I've seen television, Angel. I know what girls look like in their underwear."

"I'll meet you in the shoe store," she said calmly. She slammed the door.

As soon as she was sure he was gone, Angel ripped off the black top. She'd take the blue. The blue was not fussy, it was feminine.

As she walked toward the exit, one of the girls at the mirrors stopped her. "If you're not taking that black top, I wonder if I could just try it on," she said. "It's really fantastic."

Chapter 10
You Would Cry, Too, If It Happened to You

Sean banged on the door for at least the fifth time in forty-five minutes. "Come on, Angel," he moaned. "I really have to go."

Angel reached for the mascara with a sigh. How could her mother consider a private bathroom a luxury? Was food a luxury? Was air a luxury? Even Denise's anti-life budget didn't deny them food. So why did she think that having the space and privacy to get ready for a party without being constantly interrupted was less important than eating and breathing?

"Just hold it," Angel shouted. "I'll be out soon."

"But you said that ten minutes ago." His voice changed from moan to whine. "You've been in there for hours, and I really have to go."

She blinked as the brush came too close to her eyes. It was like trying to get dressed in a public toilet.

The door knob rattled. "Angel!"

In a public toilet that was being used as a dressing room by a passing circus. "So go in the bushes if you're so desperate."

"I'm telling Mom," Sean yelled. "You're gonna be sorry." He gave the door a kick before he thumped away.

Finished with her makeup, Angel studied herself critically in the mirror. *Not bad.* She checked each profile. *No, definitely not bad.* She could use a haircut and perm, but they, too, were on Denise's list of extravagances. Right near the top, under "own bathroom" and "own phone."

She turned to the mirror on the back of the door to view the full effect. It had taken several changes, but she'd finally decided on her short black stretch skirt. Lindy had persuaded her to buy it last winter, but she'd never actually worn it, because Gavin thought it made her look punk. But seeing the skirt matched with the new Lycra top, Angel couldn't help thinking that Gavin had been wrong. She didn't look punk. She looked great. Sixteen, but sophisticated. Stylish. She tried on a pair of her mother's long silver earrings. She looked like a model. *I am Cinderella,* she thought. *And my fairy godmother has given me a beautiful outfit, and I'm going to the ball.* Her smile brightened. She might even run into a prince. Not that she wasn't still madly in love with Gavin, of course, but you never could tell. . . .

Angel checked her watch. She was going to have to hurry if she was going to feed Sean before she left. *Cereal and soup,* she decided as she started clearing up her things. *Cornflakes and tomato soup. Fiber and fruit, you can't get more balanced than that.* It was just as she was wondering if she could give him the soup cold just this once that the horrible truth hit her like a train.

What had she been thinking of? She couldn't go to Suze's party. No way. Tonight was Denise's late night at the diner. Angel might be all dressed up, but she couldn't go. Not unless she brought Sean with her. Angel collapsed on the edge of the bathtub, weak with disappointment. This was one problem Cinderella'd never had. Maybe she'd had to clean out the fireplace and peel the potatoes, but she'd never had to baby-sit. And Angel couldn't take him. She imagined arriving with Sean at Suze's house. "Don't tell me *this* is your date!" Suze would laugh. "Is he a midget?" And Angel would say, "Oh, no. He's short, but he's not a midget. He's my brother. My mother's a career woman, you know, very high-powered. I couldn't leave him by himself, could I? He is only ten." And then Sean would run through all the rooms, looking for couples kissing in corners, shouting out, "Ohh, look, he put his tongue in her mouth! How gross!" *Go ahead, cry*, Angel told herself. *Who cares if you ruin your makeup? Who's going to see?*

Angel came slowly down the stairs. She was calm and controlled. She was also catastrophically unhappy, of course, but she was beginning to get used to it. It was her fate in life, that was all. Some girls were destined for stardom. Some for wealth. Some were even destined to work in diners. But not Angelina Camille Lister. She was destined to take care of her brother and be alone.

B.J. and Sean were sitting on the couch, watching some stupid movie, Sparky asleep between them. They were laughing. "This is the best part," Sean was saying. "Wait'll you see. It's really cool."

No one looked up as Angel stepped into the room.

She stood at the bottom of the stairs for a second, just staring at them. It wasn't fair. How dare they sit there having a good time when she was so unhappy? Rage came along and shoved her calm and control out the door. Without warning, Angel stormed across the room and snapped off the set. "Why don't you do something useful instead of watching that stupid thing all the time?" she shouted.

"What?" Sean shouted back, launching himself from the sofa and snapping the set back on. "Like spending three hours in the bathroom?"

Angel pushed him and turned it off.

Sean shoved her and turned it on.

Angel elbowed him and turned it off.

Sean threw himself against her and turned it on.

She went for his hair. She wanted to pull it out by the roots. She wanted to hear him cry. She was going to make him beg for mercy. But jut as she was about to grab hold, two strong arms closed around her and lifted her in the air.

She was too stunned to struggle. Every time William Joseph Spatano put his arms around her, she became confused. When Gavin held her, even in the most romantic circumstances, she would soon find herself thinking of other things. Once, in the back of the Corvette, she'd actually fallen asleep. But there was something about B.J. that seemed to wake her up. This close, she could smell and feel what he must have been like when he was alive. This close, she could almost forget that he wasn't.

"You really are something," said that voice in her ear. "Now, what's the matter?"

This close she could forget herself enough to think that kissing someone like William Spatano would be nothing like kissing someone like Gavin Spencer Smythe.

He shook her. "You all right, Angel? What's wrong with you?"

She couldn't help it; she started to cry.

Angel quickly pedaled Sean's bike away from Bluff Drive. Her fairy godmother provided clothes and jewelry, but she didn't stretch to a coach and horses. Angel didn't care. At least she was going to the party after all. As much as she disliked having to accept any help from B.J., this time she felt that she'd had no choice. It was either let him baby-sit or baby-sit herself. And B.J. was right, of course; she couldn't argue with his logic. It was no big deal for him. He was already there, wasn't he? And he wasn't going anywhere. He didn't have a heavy date or something else to do. He was dead, for heaven's sake. If you looked at it objectively, B.J. was lucky he had Sean to watch TV with.

So she'd let him persuade her. Did she think he couldn't fix Sean supper? Did she think he wouldn't remember to make him brush his teeth? She had hesitated. "Well . . . ," she'd said at last, "I guess it isn't really like I'm leaving him alone. . . ." The next-to-last thing B.J. said to her before she left was, "Don't worry about Sean, Angel. Just have a good time."

Angel wasn't worried about Sean. As she rode toward Suze's, Sean Lister was the last person Angel was worried about. In fact, the farther she got from home, the more she started worrying about herself. Maybe she was making a mistake. Suze was nice, she was really nice, but she was different. Different from Angel, different from Lindy, different from the kids Angel used to hang out with. B.J. liked her. No matter how nice and funny she was, the fact that B.J. liked her had to mean there was something wrong with her. A boy like that . . . everybody knew what a boy like that looked for in a girl. Angel coasted down a hill, picturing B.J. back at home with Sean, making spaghetti, popping corn for them to eat while they watched the movie. A boy like that . . .

She turned the corner. She had to be nearly there. New worries besieged her. What about Suze's friends? Would they be like Suze? At school, Suze was friendly with everyone—everyone except Silvia and May and their crowd. In the days when Angel had forced herself to go to the cafeteria, she'd noticed that Suze never sat with just one group but moved around from day to day. *Maybe she can get away with that at school,* thought Angel as she tried not to bang her knees on the handlebars, *but not at a party.* She knew from experience that you didn't mix groups socially like that. The jocks went to their parties, the rich kids went to their parties, the artsy types went to theirs, the kids like B.J. hung out in parking lots, and the droids stayed home. What if she didn't fit in with Suze's crowd? What if she hated them? She turned onto Stepple Street. What if they hated her?

Angel stopped under a streetlight to check the address. What if Suze had only asked her to this party because she felt sorry for her? The voice of B.J. Spatano floated through the night. *You're your own worst enemy*, it was saying. *You're actin' like a snob. You better cut the crap.* . . . She pulled out the paper on which she'd written down the address in the shoe store: 15 Stepple Street. The house in front of her was number 20. A new, more terrifying, thought occurred to her. What if Suze hadn't invited her out of friendship, or even out of pity? What if she'd invited her out of spite? To get even with Angel for cutting her dead in the hallway that day, to pay her back for acting like a snob? It was the kind of thing Lindy would do. It was the kind of thing Lindy had done. What if Suze had only asked her because she knew Angel would have a horrible time? *Don't be ridiculous.* Angel started pushing Sean's bike down the road. *Suze isn't like that. She's the one who's wanted to be friends. And, anyway, she'd never even thought of inviting you to this party before she saw you in the mall.* This was the first time in her life that Angel had ever taken any comfort in the idea of being forgotten. She started looking for a place to hide the bike. She didn't want everyone to know she hadn't come by car.

Fifteen Stepple Street wasn't what Angel had imagined, although, when she thought about it, she wasn't really sure what she had imagined. One of those gaudy pink houses with dead cars on the grass? Suze was so unusual that it wouldn't have surprised her. She might even live in a trailer, for all Angel knew. Angel stared at the number over the stained-glass door. Fifteen Stepple Street was old, large, full

179

of character, and beautiful in a unique kind of way. It was set on a large piece of land. Angel walked all the way back to the end of the road to make sure she really was on Stepple Street. She was. Surely there could be only one Stepple Street in a town that didn't even have its own movie house.

Angel walked quietly up to the porch and stood outside the front door. She could hear music and laughter inside. This must be the right house— either that, or everybody on Stepple Street was having a party tonight. She raised her hand to the door. *My first night out in Midville. Please let it be all right.* And then she remembered the last thing B.J. had said to her as she left the house. "You look real foxy, Angel. It's a good th— You look cool." She looked cool. She took a deep breath and rang the bell.

She had never been in a house like Suze Adams's house before. She'd seen ones something like it in the home-decorating magazines in her dentist's waiting room, but everyone she knew in Lisson Park furnished their homes from the same four or five exclusive stores, so they all looked very expensive, very tasteful, and vaguely the same. No one in Lisson Park would dream of putting a mermaid figurehead from a sailing ship beside the living room fireplace; no one there would have old church pews instead of chairs around the kitchen table.

"What an amazing place," she said as Suze showed her around. "It's so—"

"Filled with old junk," finished Suze. She led her down the basement stairs. "It's because my parents

180

are in the antiques business." She looked over her shoulder and made a face. "Can you imagine what it would be like if they were butchers or something? There'd be pigs and cows all over the house!"

Angel laughed, beginning to relax. Maybe this was going to be all right. She was here; she was laughing; Suze had complimented her on her top. Suze had said she was glad Angel had come. "Everybody's just dying to meet you," Suze had greeted her. "You know how boring it is when it's just the same old faces all the time." It didn't seem as though Suze had asked her out of spite.

Angel's eyes scanned the crowd as she and Suze descended into the crowded rec room. From what she could see, Suze's friends were as unusual as her home. Like Suze herself, they didn't seem to be one thing or another. One of the girls who had been chosen as a cheerleader when Angel had been turned down was talking to a boy with spiked orange hair. Near them, Wayne Something was passing a sponge football through his legs to the girl in Angel's English class who always dressed in purple and wrote poems about death.

Suze stopped at the bottom of the stairs, clapping her hands. "Hey, everybody!" she cried. "This is the girl who told Ms. Michaels to shut up!"

"'Bout time, too!" a familiar voice shouted back.

Angel turned. Benjy Hayman was waving to her from across the room. She was too surprised to wave back.

It felt good to feel good again. People were talking to her and laughing with her and asking for her opinion. The glances she caught from some of the guys were openly admiring. Good? It felt wonderful. Angel smiled to herself.

Jack, the boy she was dancing with, grinned back. "You should smile more. You look really nice." He moved closer. "I've wanted to meet you for ages, you know, but every time I saw you in the hall, you had this drop-dead expression on your face. . . ."

"Me?" She stared back in not totally mock surprise. "Are you sure you're not thinking of someone who looks like me?"

He laughed. "Oh, no, I'm sure of that. There's nobody else in Midville who looks like you."

Suze Adams's crowd might be as different from her own as a soy burger from a sirloin steak, but as the night went on, Angel started to think that maybe that wasn't such a bad thing. Suze had a point about the same old faces. Back home Angel had always known what to expect when she went to a party. She knew who would be there; she knew which couples were going to disappear into the make-out room; she knew who would make too much noise or spill something on the rug; most of the time she even knew what conversations she would have and with whom—the girls always talked about boys and their mothers, and the boys always talked about football, music, cars, and themselves. If things got dull, they'd turn on the computer and see what the spelling checker changed their names to: Angel Lisper, Linty Porterhouse, Gamin Scythe. But tonight she was having conversations about everything from puppet making and dirt bikes to bats and rhythm and blues. Jack, in fact, was not only a pretty good dancer, he

182

was a fund of information on hot-air balloons.

I can't believe this, Angel thought as she spun around. *I really am happy. I really am having a good time.*

The song ended, and they went to stand against the wall, near the snack table.

Jack passed her the bowl of pretzels. "My brother's picking me up soon," he said. "You want a ride home?"

She was so happy that she almost said yes. But then she remembered Sean's bike, under the bushes of 17 Stepple Street.

"Oh, thanks," she said quickly. "But I— My mother's coming for me."

He shrugged. "You could call her and save her the trip."

Leave the bike, a little voice advised her. *You can always get it tomorrow. Who wants to pedal home in the dark when you could be driving in a nice, warm car with a nice, warm boy?* Not Angel Lister, that was for sure.

"Well, I'm not—"

"Come on," Jack coaxed. "If I know where you live, then I'll know where to pick you up when we go on our first date."

She stared at him. And thought of Gavin. Of course she couldn't go out with Jack, not when Gavin, brokenhearted, was waiting for her to return to Lisson Park. Jack was cute. Jack was smart. Jack was fun. But she couldn't go out with him. Could she?

Jack grinned, leaning his head against hers. "Does that look mean yes or no?"

She pictured Jack walking up the drive to her house. Past the iridescent van with the words BLUE MOON DINER stenciled on the side. Up to the sagging porch. Into the dingy living room, where her brother would be lying on the couch, bored and waiting to be entertained. Or, even worse, playing backgammon with B.J. That should impress Jack. And, besides, unless Jack only asked her out on Sunday afternoons, they'd never be able to go anywhere that Sean wouldn't want to go with them. Unless he lived in a slum himself, he'd be horrified by the place she called home. She looked around the room. The Adams's finished basement was practically bigger than their whole house. How could she let any of these kids know where she lived? She must have been temporarily insane to think she could come here and make friends. And then do what with them? Only meet them in town on days when the diner was closed, so she wouldn't have to worry about running into her mother with her MY NAME'S DENISE, I'M HERE TO SERVE YOU tag on her blouse.

Angel looked at her watch. "Oh, my God!" she exclaimed. "I didn't know it was so late. My mother's probably outside right now." She headed for the stairs. "I really have to go, Jack. I'll see you Monday."

"Wait a minute!" He followed her as she made her way through the crowd. "What about tomorrow? Couldn't we do something tomorrow?"

She reached the stairs and picked up speed. "Not tomorrow. Tomorrow I'm busy. But I'll see you in school. Maybe we could have lunch."

He pounded after her. "But couldn't we at least talk on the phone? Give me your number, and I'll call."

How was she going to get rid of him? "Sure," said Angel, thinking fast. For the first time she felt she really understood what that old saying "Necessity is the mother of invention" meant. It meant desperate times called for desperate actions. "Sure. Just wait right here, okay? I have to use the bathroom."

"Deal." Jack parked himself on the landing. "I won't move."

She could only pray that he didn't. She walked down the hallway to the bathroom. At the bathroom door, however, she paused and glanced over her shoulder. Jack was talking to someone and not looking in her direction. She went past the bathroom, into the kitchen, and straight out the back door.

Angel was beginning to learn that life was full of surprises. It didn't pay to make assumptions. She'd assumed she'd live in Lisson Park until she went away to college. She'd assumed that Suze Adams wasn't the sort of person she would like as a friend. She'd assumed her mother would be sleeping by the time she got home, and that she could tiptoe up to her room and fall asleep wondering whether she would have gone out with Jack if there were no Gavin, no Sean, and no 52 Bluff Drive—and if she might not go out with him anyway.

Sleeping? Her mother wasn't even tired.

Angel was locking Sean's bike on the porch when

the front door was suddenly jerked open with such violence that Angel jumped. Her mother, still in her work clothes, was framed in the doorway. She didn't look happy. Angel thought about saying something—hi, or hello, something like that—but Denise didn't give her a chance. "What do you call this?" she screamed. "Just what do you think you're doing?"

Angel was so surprised by this unexpected attack that she said the wrong thing. "I'm locking up the bike."

Her mother grabbed her by the arm and yanked her into the house. "Don't you get smart with me, young lady," she shouted.

"But Mom, I—"

"Don't 'but Mom' me!" She shoved Angel into the living room. "I leave you in charge of the house. I leave you to take care of your brother. I think I can trust you . . . and what do you do? Huh? What do you do?"

Angel backed out of her mother's way. "But Mom, I left you a note explaining. I—"

"You go to a party, that's what you do! You steal money from me to buy yourself clothes you don't need and were told you can't have, and you go to a party. I have never heard of anything so irresponsible and so selfish before in my life."

Sean Diarrhea-of-the-Mouth Lister, thought Angel. *Just wait till I get my hands on you, you little cretin. You're going to be lucky if you ever see eleven.*

"But, Mom, I didn't steal the money. I'm going to pay it back, with inter—"

Denise rolled on like a runaway tank. "That

money was for Sean, not for you, Angel, and you knew it! You knew it, and you took it anyway!"

Angel couldn't remember when she'd seen her mother this angry before. Her father was always shouting and complaining about something, but not Denise. She was the calm one, the one who took care of everything, the one who always tried to understand.

"But Sean said it was okay. Sean said—"

"And that's not even the worst of it!" Denise raged. "That's nothing. Not only do you take money from your little brother, you leave him alone as well! Ten!" she screamed. "He's only ten!" She folded her arms over her chest and stared into Angel's face. "Have you completely lost your mind? Don't you have any sense of responsibility?" She shook her head in disbelief and disappointment. "I know you're spoiled and selfish, Angel, but to leave your brother all by himself— What if something had happened? Did you think of that? What if he were hurt or ill, or there was an accident?"

Tears of indignation trickled down Angel's cheeks. How unfair could you get? "But I didn't leave him alone!" she protested. "B.J. was with him. B.J. may be obnoxious, but he can take care of anything."

The effect of those words on her mother—words meant to let Denise know exactly how unjust she was being—was immediate and total. It was as though someone had unplugged her. She stood gawking at Angel, apparently unable to speak.

Foolishly, Angel took this as a good sign. She wiped her eyes with her sleeve. "I wouldn't leave

Sean all alone, Mom. You know that. And, anyway, it was BJ's idea. B.J. said that since he was here anyway—"

Someone put the plug back in. "Let me get this straight," her mother interrupted. "You go off and leave a ten-year-old boy all by himself, and you expect me to buy that it was okay for you to do that because you left him with a kid who's been dead since the fifties?"

"He is nineteen, and he's very mature in a sort of barbaric way. And if you count all the years he's been dead, he's even older than you."

Denise wasn't counting. "I don't know what you think you're doing, Angel, encouraging Sean in these fantasies. I've told you how worried I am about him, but you still insist on going along with it. Maybe you think you can manipulate him more by convincing him there's a ghost. Maybe you think if his problem gets serious enough, we really will move back to Maryland. . . ."

"But Mom, I never thought that. I told you before, B.J. really—"

Denise's voice was like an Arctic night. "Knowing you," she went on, "I'm sure you have it all worked out to your advantage."

Angel felt as though she'd been slapped in the face. "That's not fair. That—"

"But it stops now, Angel. Do you hear me? If there's one more word out of your mouth about this ghost, I'm going to give every stitch of clothes you own to the Salvation Army. Is that clear?"

Clear as just-washed glass. Everyone and everything was against her. She couldn't even have a few meager hours of happiness without being punished for it. She couldn't do anything right. Her own mother had turned against her.

"Why wait?" Angel screamed back. "Why not just give them to them now? Why not give them everything I own? You don't care about me. All you care about are yourself and Sean." The words tumbled out on top of one another with a will of their own. "You've destroyed my life," Angel sobbed, "and you don't even know it. You don't ever think of me. You don't ever worry about me. Here I am stuck in this dump every day, and you don't give it a thought. I can't go anywhere or do anything because I have to look after Sean and the house. Oh, poor little Sean. Make sure he has his lunch, make sure he does his homework, make sure he has new shoes. But not you, Angel. You can't have anything new. Just Sean. SeanSeanSeanSean!" Angel couldn't stop shaking, she was crying so much. "I don't have anything. I don't have any friends, I don't have any time for myself, all I have is nothing. But you don't care! The only reason you even brought me with you is so you'd have somebody to do all your work for you and mind your little brat!" She ran past her mother and up the stairs.

"Angel!" Denise called after her. "Angel! You come back here!"

The attic door slammed closed.

"Whew," breathed Sean after Angel stormed through their room and up to her own. "I've never heard Mom get so mad before."

The glow of B.J.'s cigarette shone from the opposite bed. "She's tired, that's all. She's had a long day. By tomorrow it'll all be forgotten."

"Are you sure?" Sean asked. He sounded worried. "I don't think I've ever heard Angel so upset, either. It sort of scares me, B.J. I wasn't going to tell Mom about the sneakers, you know that, but she asked me. What else could I do?"

A genie-like wisp of smoke shimmered in the light from the window. "It's not your fault," said B.J. "It's nobody's fault. Lots of times things are nobody's fault—they just happen."

"But what about Angel?" asked Sean. His eyes moved to the ceiling. "Listen to her, B.J. Do you think she's all right?"

B.J.'s eyes, too, were on the ceiling. "At least it looks like she's stopped throwing things around for awhile," he answered. "She'll probably fall asleep soon."

"Me, too," said Sean. He pulled the covers up around him and rolled on his side. "You know what, B.J.?"

B.J. kept watching the space above his head, as though able to see through lathe and plaster. "No, what?"

"That was the best meal I've had since Angel started cooking."

"It's practically the only meal you've had since Angel started cooking. I don't count cereal and canned soup, myself."

"No, really," Sean said, "it was good."

"I'm glad you liked it," B.J. replied, but his ears were straining to hear Denise as she came up the stairs. She came so quietly, you'd think she was sneaking in after curfew. Very gently, she opened the door to her room; very softly, she shut it again. Almost immediately, the radio came on. Denise never played the radio at night. He guessed it was so they wouldn't hear her crying. Angel's sobs, on the other hand, drifted down through the walls.

"B.J.?" Sean asked sleepily. "B.J., you're really sure it'll be all right, aren't you?"

"Sure I'm sure." He leaned against the window. "I'm positive."

It was only after Sean was asleep that B.J. climbed outside to get away from the unhappy sounds of the house. He wasn't as positive as he had tried to sound that everything would be all right in the morning. He wasn't sure at all. *Man,* he said to himself. *It's been a long, long time since I saw two people that unhappy. Or that mad.* He sat down in the recess of the roof.

It was a cool night with a moon like a slice of melon. It was a night to be young on; a night to be in love. B.J. had been young, and once he'd even been in love, but mainly he'd been unhappy and mad. He rested his back against the house, remembering himself alive and up in the room where Angel was weeping. On a night like this—on any night—chances were he would've been sitting there in the dark, crazy with rage. He'd never cried. He'd hit things, or he'd listened to music until his old man threatened to bust the door down, or he'd disappeared on his bike, but he'd never cried. It was like there'd been a wall between him and everybody else. Everybody except his brother Danny. Danny, he loved. He'd always done everything he could for Danny. Too much, maybe. But everybody else he'd hated. The wall had gotten bigger and thicker, and he'd hated them more and more. If only there had been some way of tearing down that wall. Or at least of punching a hole through it. Then maybe things would've turned out differently. He was suddenly aware of the silence; Angel must have fallen asleep. *What about* their *wall?* he wondered. *What about the wall between Angel and Denise?*

B.J. gazed up at the sky. It was a night when you might wish upon a star, as well. B.J. wished.

Chapter 11
Little Runaway

Well, I don't care anymore, either, Angel thought angrily. *I don't care what happens to my mother; I don't care what happens to Sean. They can just get along without me from now on.* She rolled on her other side, facing the wall.

Although it was well past noon, Angel was still in her pajamas and still in bed, thinking about the unfairness of life. Downstairs, she could hear Sean and Denise talking, laughing, and watching TV as though everything were all right. Angel didn't care about that, either. And she didn't care that Denise had closed the diner for the whole of Sunday and stayed home to try to coax her out of her room. Several times, Denise had knocked on the door or shouted up the stairs, wanting her to come and watch the video, or play Risk with her and Sean, or eat, but Angel hadn't even shouted back, "Go away!" There would be no more lazy Sunday afternoons as far as she was concerned. No more going to the movies together or playing board games till midnight or laughing so hard over some silly joke that they all had tears in their eyes. Angel Lister had had enough.

Angel sat up. First her mother treated her like a servant, and now she was treating her like a criminal. The injustice of her mother's attack—accusing her of the one thing she hadn't done, leaving Sean alone—kept coming back to her. *That's what you get for being selfless,* she told herself. *You get more trouble.* She stared out the window. The sky was dark with gathering clouds. It looked the way she felt. Just when she thought things were going to be all right, that it was a sunny day after all, everything went black again. *Well, I'm not going to live like this,* Angel told herself. *That's for sure. Not any more.*

The clatter of pots and slamming of cabinets announced that Denise was fixing Sunday dinner. *I hope she trips over something,* thought Angel. *I hope the toaster explodes.* Now she really didn't care, because she knew what she was going to do. Leave. She couldn't believe she hadn't thought of it sooner. She didn't have to stay where she wasn't wanted, where she wasn't appreciated or understood. Not when there was a place where she *was* wanted. A place where everyone understood and appreciated her. A place where she was loved. She scowled as B.J. Spatano appeared in the backyard, strolling across the lawn with his collar up and his filthy mutt running ahead of him. Lisson Grove, Maryland, place of beautiful homes and beautiful people—and no ghosts.

She would go home. She had more than enough in her savings account to buy a train ticket to Maryland, and as soon as the bank opened in the morning, she was going to withdraw it and do just that. Denise thought she was spoiled, selfish, and irresponsible? Well, they'd just see how easy Denise found it without her around. Who'd look after the house and Sean then? The thought of Denise regretting forever the awful way she'd treated her only daughter finally made Angel smile.

Turning from the window, she jumped to her feet. Now that she knew what to do, she wanted to get started. She dragged her bright pink carryall down from the shelf in her closet. *Now, don't go overboard,* she advised herself. *Just take the bare necessities for now, and you can send for the rest later.* She started pulling things out of her closet and dresser and throwing them on the bed. She was still deciding which things she couldn't live without for even a week and imagining how happy everyone was going to be to see her again when her mother's voice interrupted her thoughts.

"Angel!" Denise called from the living room. "Angel!"

Angel jammed her diary and her pink mohair sweater into the bag.

"Angel, don't you want some dinner? I'm making your favorite potatoes. Aren't you coming down?"

"When girls with thick thighs model bathing suits," Angel muttered. "That's when I'll come down." She squeezed in another pair of shoes.

"Why don't you give her a break? She's tryin' to patch it up."

Angel swung around. She'd dragged the dresser in front of the door, to make sure that Denise couldn't get in, and B.J. was leaning against it, his

195

eyes on her. He hadn't taken a very long walk.

"I hate the way you do that," she snapped. "I really wish you'd learn to knock."

"Why don't you just go downstairs and apologize to your mom? Don't she have enough on her mind without having to worry about you, too?"

He couldn't even speak English properly, and he was trying to tell her what to do. *"Me? Me* apologize? She's the one who should be apologizing. She's the one who was wrong."

"You don't think maybe you're both a little wrong?"

"Me?" she shrieked. "What about *you?* You're the one who had the bright idea. None of this would have happened if it weren't for you!"

But B.J. Spatano, of course, was not a boy to take the blame for anything. He threw himself on the bed next to her carryall and changed the subject.

"Look, let's be reasonable, okay? Denise knows things have been unfair on you, Angel. She sees that now." He started fiddling with the strap of her bag. "So why don't you give her a chance to make it up? Why don't you at least talk to her and see what happens?"

"Why don't you mind your own business for a change and see what happens?" She rolled her brocade jacket into a tube and pushed it into a tightly packed corner.

B.J. started poking through the things on the bed. "Look," he said slowly, "y'both said stuff last night when you were mad that you didn't really mean—"

Angel grabbed her hair dryer out of his hand and

moved her possessions out of his reach. "It just so happens, Mr. Fix-it, that I meant every single word I said last night."

"Get off it, Angel. You were up—"

"I am *out*. That's what I am, out."

"Out?" For the first time he seemed to understand that what she was doing was packing. He stared at the carryall. "What are y'talkin' about, *out?*"

"You know," said Angel. "*Out. As in out of here.*" With some effort, she started to wrench the zipper closed. "Like, I'm splitting, man. Like, I'm gone. Like, I'm not going to be here to be pushed around anymore. So you can have your stupid room back, and I hope you're very happy in it." She snuffed back a tear. "You're bound to be happier than I've been."

"Have you gone completely nuts? You can't leave. Where are y'goin'?"

"I'm going home."

"Home? But you *are* home."

She gave him one of her biggest and most insincere smiles. "I do not have to live like this," she said in her clearest voice. "Stuck in an attic with a dead juvenile delinquent. Treated like Cinderella." She threw a handful of tapes into a side pocket and snapped it closed. "My father will give me anything I want. Clothes, money, my own phone . . . anything." She dragged the bag to the floor with a grunt. "And he won't expect me to do the laundry or stay home all the time, either."

He was staring at her with a look that Angel thought must be awe.

197

But it wasn't. "You're gonna leave Denise and Sean?" It was simple stupefaction. "You're goin' back to Listerine Park?"

He wasn't just a juvenile delinquent. He was a *juvenile* juvenile delinquent. "You can call it whatever you want," said Angel. "But it's ten million times better than this dump."

He shook his head. "You're makin' a mistake, Angel. You can't go back. This is your home now. With your mom and Sean. They're your family."

Mr. Wreck-on-the-Highway, he should talk. "My father's my family." She turned her back on him and started going through her dresser one last time. "My mistake was not staying with him in Lisson Park."

B.J. slid off the bed and came to where she was standing. "Look, you're upset. You have a right to be upset. But just talk to your mom before you do something stupid." He laid a hand on her arm. "She really is sorry, Angel. I know she is. Just give her a chance."

She stepped around him. He was trying to make her look at him, but she wouldn't. When he came to one side, she turned to the other.

"I'm not talking to her about anything, ever again." She pushed in the top drawer so hard that the plastic Eiffel Tower her mother had brought back for her from Paris seven years before fell on the floor. Angel didn't pick it up.

"Will y'listen, for Pete's sake? She knows she was hard on you. She cried all night, too, Angel. Maybe if you'd just—"

He was lying, as usual. Denise never cried about

198

anything. "Maybe if you'd just haunt someone else for a change, I could finish my packing." She squatted down to make sure she hadn't left anything vital in the bottom drawer.

He squatted beside her. "Look me in the eyes and tell me you know you're not making a mistake. I dare you. Look me in the eyes."

She looked him in the eyes. It was like looking into the moonless night. "I know what I'm doing."

He didn't seem too convinced. "Now where have I heard that before?" he asked.

B.J. sat on the railing of the porch, watching the wind blow the leaves across the yards and the first drops of rain hit the asphalt. He'd been standing there all night, thinking, and now here it was, Monday morning, and he was still there, and still thinking.

To squeal or not to squeal, that was always the question.

It had been the question with his brother Danny. As far as Renee and his father had been concerned, Danny had been born perfect and got better. "Why can't you be more like your brother?" the old man had always been after him. Danny's so good at school, Danny's so polite, Danny's so normal, so nice, such a credit to his family and the human race. "I can be proud of Danny," the old man had always told him. "Not like you. You're not fit to live." Danny this and Danny that, it was all he'd ever heard. Danny was Renee's and the old man's son, but not B.J.—B.J. was the son of the dead woman, born with a chip on his shoulder. Born to be bad.

But the funny thing was, even though Danny was always being shoved in his face, B.J. had always loved him. His little brother. His. He'd been only three when Danny was born, but he could still remember Renee bringing Danny home from the hospital, and himself standing by the bassinet and thinking, *That's my brother!* "Don't touch him," Renee had warned. "You'll give him germs." And it was true: he had given him germs. He'd given Danny the measles and the chicken pox, but he'd given him more than that. He'd watched out for him. He'd protected him. He'd taken the blame. Renee and the old man had always spoiled Danny, but B.J. hadn't cared. It had been as if he'd thought Danny had had a right to be spoiled, to be safe from the anger and the arguments. If Danny didn't do his homework, B.J. had done it for him. If someone picked a fight with Danny, B.J. had fought it. Danny was his brother. In a house where no one else had wanted him, Danny had. Danny had needed him.

So even when Danny had started running around with the wrong crowd, B.J. had kept quiet. Even when he'd known that Danny was sneaking out at night to hang out on the streets, he'd never said anything. To squeal or not to squeal. The old man wouldn't have believed him, anyway. "Danny?" Danny joy-riding? Danny lying? Danny stealing? Danny creeping home at three in the morning, stinking of beer? "You lyin' punk. God should strike you down," the old man would have said. But that hadn't been the reason B.J. didn't tell. It was because he'd thought he could handle it. He could keep Danny safe. Even when B.J. had found out about the robbery at the liquor store, even then he had thought he could handle it, make it all right. He could save his brother, just like he'd always done before.

To squeal or not to squeal. And all these years later, it was the same question again. Should he let Angel run away, or should he stop her by warning Denise through Sean?

Sean came out the door in his windbreaker, his book bag over his shoulder. "Can you believe it?" he asked, indignant. "Angel won't let me take my bike because it's going to rain. You'd think I was a little kid or something." He clumped down the stairs. "See you later, B.J." He waved as he marched across the lawn.

You can still run after him, B.J. told himself as Sean headed in the direction of the bus stop. *It isn't too late.*

But he knew he wouldn't. He hadn't been able to do it thirty-odd years ago, and he couldn't do it now. It was too much like being a stool pigeon.

As soon as Sean was out of sight, B.J. heard Angel lugging her carryall down the stairs. He turned to watch her drag it out the front door.

"Look, princess," he said, stepping out of her way. "Don't y'think you should wait? It really is going to rain, you know. There are storm warnings up and down the coast."

She bounced the carryall down the porch steps.

"What if your father's not home?" He followed her to the garage. "What if he's out of town or somethin'? At least wait till the weather's clear."

"You're just trying to scare me." She strapped

her bag on the back of Sean's bike. "But it won't work. I'm leaving, and there's nothing you can do to stop me."

Not just stubborn, infuriating. She was the most infuriating girl he'd ever known.

"I'm not just sayin' it. Turn on the radio and hear for yourself. They're talkin' about hurricanes."

Angel gave him one of her don't-even-try-to-lick-my-shoes looks. "Hurricanes?"

"Yeah, hurricanes. I know everything's perfect in Listerine Park, your majesty, but even there you must have heard of bad weather."

"You are pathetic." She straddled the bike. "You are absolutely pathetic. After all I've been through, do you think a little rain is going to scare me?"

He grabbed the handlebars. "It's never a good idea to surprise people, Angel. At least call your old man first. Make sure he's expectin' you."

"*My* father loves me," said Angel. "I don't have to call for an appointment.

She really knew how to make him feel small. You'd think she knew his father wouldn't have given a dime for him. That if he'd made an appointment with his father, the old man would have broken it.

B.J. stepped back. "Suit yourself," he said. "You're the ruling monarch."

"And you're the court jester," she snapped as she pedaled away.

By noon the rain was heavier and the wind was shaking the trees and tossing garbage cans down the road. Sparky was lying by the front door, his

202

ears down, moaning. B.J. turned on the radio.

"She'll be back," he reassured Sparky. "She's mad, but she ain't stupid." He stared out the window at the storm of leaves and the twisting trees. "Well, not *that* stupid. She'll get halfway to the train and realize she's actin' like a jerk."

Sean came home twenty minutes later. "Hey, guess what?" he screamed, racing into the house. "They let us off early because of the hurricane! Isn't it neat, B.J.? Everybody says the lights will go off."

B.J. didn't move his eyes from the TV screen, where film clips of the hurricane's devastation in Florida were being shown—cars floating in what looked like lakes, houses with their roofs torn off. Pretty young girls with bloodied, tear-stained faces being helped into ambulances.

Sean leaned over the sofa. "Hey, B.J. What's up? Why are you listening to the radio and the television at the same time?"

B.J. clicked off the remote control and took his feet from the coffee table. "Just checkin' the weather." He took his jacket from the back of the couch. "I think I'll take a look down the road," he said, trying to sound casual. "See if Angel's comin'. If they sent you home, they must've sent her home, too."

Sean gaped at him as though he'd lost a wheel. "You're kidding, right? You're going to meet Angel at the bus? What for?"

Now, there was a question: why? He nodded out the window. "She didn't take her umbrella."

The thunderstruck expression stayed on Sean's

face. "Take her an umbrella? You want to go out in the rain to take Angel an umbrella? B.J., she hates you. She'd rather get wet. Geez, she'd rather drown."

B.J. stood up. "Yeah, maybe . . . but I think I'll just go down t'the corner. She's havin' enough trouble with your mom. She doesn't need pneumonia, too." He grabbed Angel's umbrella from the closet and strode through the door, whistling for Sparky to follow him. But Sparky hated storms. He refused to budge.

B.J. left the umbrella on the porch. He walked slowly to the end of Bluff Drive, his eyes on the slick road that led to town. There was no sign of a dark-haired girl on a small blue bike. No sign of a dark-haired girl on foot, dragging a pink bag behind her. He knew she wouldn't be on the bus. He scanned the sky. The clouds made him think of the motor oil stains on the floor of the garage. *Okay*, he told himself. *Okay, if she isn't back by now, she must've got as far as New York. But she won't know her way around the city. She'll be scared. She'll come home.* He hunched inside his jacket and started back to the house. Yeah, that was what she'd do. She'd get to New York, and then she'd come back. Be home in time for supper.

From somewhere on the block a cat howled. B.J. didn't like cats. There'd been a cat at the liquor store that night, the night of the robbery. A big, black cat. An omen.

Maybe he should have gone after her this morning. Followed her, made her listen to reason. Not that anyone could make Angel Lister listen to

204

reason. He jammed his hands in his pockets. And, anyway, going after her would have meant taking the Vincent out on the road. It'd been too long. Too long, and he couldn't ride in the rain. He couldn't even think of it. He'd rather ride through hell.

Sean looked up as B.J. returned. "So what's the big deal?" he asked, noticing the look on B.J.'s face. "She probably went to that girl's house. You know, the one who had the party." He turned back to the set. "She'll be home soon. She hates to be out in the rain. It frizzes her hair."

B.J. was looking at Sean, but he was seeing Danny. Danny sitting in the passenger seat of a pale blue Chevy. Danny was leaning out the window with a cocky grin. "Don't worry, man," Danny was saying. "You go on. I'll see y'soon."

B.J. threw his jacket on a chair. It happened that people never came back. It happened all the time.

"I'm afraid no one's available to take your call right now," said Marshall Lister's deep, melodious voice. "After the tone, please leave your name, number, and the time you called."

"Daddy?" said Angel. "Daddy, are you there? It's me, Angel." She held her breath, expecting her father to snatch up the receiver. "Daddy? I'm in Maryland. I'm at the train station." Surely, even if he were in the middle of dinner or something, he would pick up now. "Daddy, I guess you're not there." He might be taking a shower. Maybe if she spoke louder . . . "I'm taking a bus, Daddy!" Maybe if she shouted. "I'm at the train station,

205

Daddy, and I'm taking a bus!" Nothing. "I'll be there soon, I guess," she screamed, holding on for a second longer, just in case he was running to the phone from the bath.

Angel slammed down the receiver and picked up her bag. It had been an awful trip. She'd missed the first train to the city by minutes and had had to wait nearly two hours for the next one. When she'd gotten to New York, she'd gone to Grand Central Station instead of Penn Station. She hated New York. Everyone looked either angry or threatening. She'd been too scared to ask anyone for directions, afraid that they'd rob her or attack her or worse. When she finally reached Penn Station, her heart pounding and her whole body soaked, she'd discovered that the fare was more than she'd thought. To cover the ticket had taken all the extra money she'd counted on for food and a cab in case her father didn't meet her at the station. And now this. Her father's voice, but not her father. Where was he? He should be home by now. Angel schlumped toward the sign that read BUSES— toward the sound of steady rain. As she left the train station, B.J. Spatano's voice started talking in her head. *What if he's away?* it was saying. *What if he isn't home?* A passing taxi sprayed her as she searched for the bus that would take her near her father's new apartment. *Maybe you should wait for the weather to clear,* said B.J.'s voice. *Maybe you shouldn't surprise him.* "Oh, shut up, you moron," she said aloud. "Aren't things bad enough?"

Sean was standing beside him, watching every

move. "How come I'm eating so early?" he asked.

"I thought you said y'were hungry?"

Sean picked at the cheese. "Yeah, I *am* hungry. But Angel never gives me supper till—"

"Well, Angel ain't here right now, is she?" As though you couldn't notice that she wasn't here. As though he'd been able to think of anything else all afternoon.

Sean took another piece of cheese. "You don't have to go to all this trouble, you know," Sean said. "I mean, that stuff you made me the other night was great, but I don't care, really. I'm used to soup and cereal for supper."

B.J. flipped the omelette over. The reason Sean was eating so early was to give B.J. something to do. It kept him from thinking too much. "Yeah, well, Angel is not Betty Crocker, that's for sure." She was a lot of things, but no cook. He stirred the potatoes. She was a pain in the butt, that's what she was. Why did he bother worrying about her. "Get out the ketchup. You can't eat a western and home fries without ketchup."

Sean threw himself at the refrigerator. "Do you think the hurricane will hit us soon?" He opened the door. "Do you think it'll knock out the electricity?"

"It looks like we'll probably miss the worst," said B.J. "But it still don't sound too good." It didn't sound too good at all. He was careful not to glance out the window as something hit the garage. There was flooding down the coast, and several major roads had been closed. They were setting up emergency shelters from the Carolinas to New

207

York. The last time he'd seen anything like this had been the last time he'd seen anything at all.

"Oh, boy, I hope the lights *do* go out," said Sean excitedly. "Wouldn't that be cool, B.J.?" He landed in his chair. "Maybe after supper we should get the flashlights out. Just in case."

B.J., listening more to the radio on the counter than to Sean, slid the omelette onto a plate. "It couldn't hurt." If Angel had reached her father's— and she must have reached her father's by now— then why didn't she call? Why didn't her father make her phone home so they wouldn't worry? "We better make sure nothing's been left on the porch, too."

Sean sniffed at his food. "How come the potatoes are red? Are they supposed to be red?"

B.J. slapped him on the back of the head. "Where were you raised? Of course they're supposed t'be red. That's the way they make them in all the best diners. I bet that's the way your mom makes them at the Blue Moon."

And a father who was concerned about his daughter was supposed to make sure that her mother knew she was all right. Unless, that was, the father in question wasn't that concerned. Or unless the daughter in question had never made it to her father's house. His back to the window, B.J. listened to the wind and rain ripping at the house, tearing apart the night. He couldn't take the Vincent on the road. He couldn't ride in a storm. But he couldn't shake the feeling that Angel was in trouble. Sparky howled as though his heart would break. Maybe he hadn't been able to keep Danny

208

out of trouble, but that didn't mean that he couldn't keep Angel out.

B.J. put his hands on the back of Sean's chair and pulled it back so suddenly that Sean screamed. "Hey! B.J., what are you doing?"

"I think maybe you better call your mother."

Sean looked around in bewilderment, his fork almost at his mouth. "Now?"

"Uh huh. Now. Call her and ask her if she's heard from your dad."

Sean groaned. "Can't it wait till I eat?"

In answer, B.J. lifted him up and carried him into the living room. "Geez, B.J.," Sean protested, "what's wrong with you?"

He set him down by the phone. "Call her."

"She'll think I'm crazy."

"She knows you're crazy. Just call her."

Puzzled, but more obedient than Angel would have been, Sean dialed the number of the diner. B.J. started putting on his jacket while Sean waited for Denise to come to the phone.

"Mom?" said Sean at last, his eyes on B.J. "Mom, it's me. Mom, I know this sounds weird, but has Dad called you?"

B.J. stopped at the door.

"No reason, Mom. I was just— Could you hang on a minute?" He put his hand over the mouthpiece. "Hey! Where are you going?"

"I'm goin' after your sister."

"Now? But it's night. And it's raining."

"It's all right, I'm takin' my bike."

Sean stared at him.

"Sean?" Denise's voice, loud and slightly shrill,

drifted into their silence. "Sean? What are you up to? Where's Angel? What's going on?"

B.J. pointed to the telephone. "Tell her Angel's run away," he ordered. "Tell her to call your old man. Pronto."

"But, B.J.—"

B.J. ripped Marshall Lister's new address from the bulletin board on his way through the kitchen. He stuffed it into his jacket pocket.

Sean's voice tailed him to the door. "You better call Dad," he was saying. "Angel's run away."

B.J. wheeled the Vincent out of the garage into the black, tormented night. The wind wound round the corners of the house, sounding like ninety on a wet road. And then, as he climbed on the bike, he heard that other sound, long and low and lonely. He started the engine and roared off. Leaving Sparky howling at the kitchen door.

Angel held her finger on the bell and counted to three. She let go, and leaned her head against the door again. Definitely. She could definitely hear noises inside. Music. Voices. Why wasn't he answering? What on earth could he be doing that was more important than letting her in? This time she held the bell to the count of five.

"Stop that damn racket!" yelled her father. It was not the deep, melodious voice on the answering machine, the voice he used for his patients. It was his at-home voice, impatient and annoyed. "This better be important," he was saying as he opened the door.

"Daddy!"

It had been a lousy day and a lousy trip, and Angel felt like she had when she was four and got lost in a big department store and thought she would never see her parents again. She still remembered standing there in a canyon of crystal glasses, terrified to move, and then suddenly seeing her father striding toward her with his arms open. She couldn't help it. At the sight of her father, she burst into tears.

Angel thought he would be so horrified at the sight of her—wet and dirty, tired and hungry, mistreated by her mother, unfairly accused of wrongs she hadn't committed—that he would scoop her up in his arms the way he had when she was four and carry her inside. All during the interminable bus ride she had imagined him saying, "My child! What have they done to you? Thank God you're home! Home at last!"

"Angel," said her father, for some reason sounding more nervous than horrified. "Angel, honey, what are you doing here?" He leaned out to look down the hall. "Where's your mother?"

"Daddy!" Angel repeated. She flung herself into his arms. "Daddy, I'm so glad to see you! It was horrible, it was so awful . . . oh, Daddy, I'm so glad I'm home."

"Well . . . Angel . . . well, honey . . ." Something light and tentative touched her back; her father's hand. "Well, I'm glad to see you, too." He laughed, pushing her an inch or two away to look at her face. "Your mother isn't with you?"

Angel shook her head, trying to get the whole heartbreaking story out at once and mainly managing to snuffle and sob. "No . . . she . . . I came by myself," she finally said.

Marshall gingerly put his arm around her shoulder. "My God, you're soaking wet!" He seemed surprised. "You'd better come inside."

By the time she had taken off her jacket and her shoes, and her father had gotten her some tissues and the hand towel from the kitchen, Angel had begun to notice that something was wrong. Sitting on her father's new white leather couch, she looked at him. He wasn't wearing socks or shoes, and his shirt was misbuttoned, as though he had thrown his clothes on in a hurry. He sat on the edge of the sofa's matching armchair, smiling and tapping the leather with his fingertips, his eyes darting frequently to the door to the bedroom behind her. She could almost swear that she heard the shower running. As tired and upset as she was, it began to occur to her that this was not the welcome she'd expected. Her father was not unconditionally delighted to see her. She wasn't sure that he was even a little delighted to see her.

Angel blew her nose and wiped the last few hundred tears away.

"Better?" her father asked hopefully.

Angel nodded.

Marshall looked at his watch. He looked back at Angel and smiled. "So tell me what this is all about," he said, as though she'd come complaining of headaches. "Why aren't you at home?"

What was wrong with him? Why did he seem so distracted? Why didn't he understand why she was there? Angel started crying again. "But I *am*

212

home," she sobbed. "That's what I've been trying to tell you. I'm never going back to Midville again." Choking on her tears, she poured out the whole story. How she hated the house and the town and school. How Denise hardly had any time for them, how she made Angel do all the work, how Angel never had any time for herself. "That's why I decided to move back with you," she sobbed. "I should never have left. This is where I belong."

"Darling?" called a woman's voice from the bedroom. "Darling, who was at the door?"

Chapter 12
You Can Never Go Home Again

Take my advice. Don't surprise people. It's always a mistake. Angel sat on the sofa, listening to her father offer her a shower and a frozen dinner, hearing B.J.'s voice. She heard it while Marshall was explaining his new life to her. She heard it while he was introducing Zena to her. She heard it while Zena was offering her a shower and a frozen dinner, and reminding Marshall that they were going to be late for the Swansons. *Don't surprise people, Angel. It's always a mistake.*

Except that she was the one who was surprised. Angel had never really thought about why her parents had decided to divorce. When she'd thought about her father, back in Maryland, she'd imagined him as he had been when they all lived together. She'd assumed he was waiting for them to come back. She'd never thought of him on his own, doing different things, seeing different people, leading a different life. She had never considered that, like her mother, he might want to start all over. And not just with a new apartment and a white leather couch—that he might have wanted to start over with a new marriage as well.

While Zena put the dinner in the microwave, Angel took a shower and changed into dry clothes.

What a fool she'd been. She'd convinced herself that her father was against their leaving Lisson Park, that he'd wanted them close, when all along the opposite had been true. He'd probably been so happy when Denise said she was moving them to Long Island that it was a wonder he hadn't driven them up himself. At least now she understood why she'd heard so little from her father since they'd moved away. He'd been busy. Getting his life restarted. Making plans. Falling in love. "I haven't even had a chance to tell your mother," he'd said, his arm around Zena. "It happened so fast." *Fast!* thought Angel. *Fast! Fast is for horses. There isn't a horse in the world who would behave like this.*

When she came out of the bathroom, her father was shrugging and hanging up the receiver.

"I can't get hold of your mother," he said. "The phone's dead."

Angel felt her heart sink a little lower with disappointment. She hadn't admitted it to herself, but she'd been looking forward to hearing her mother's voice.

Zena came in with Angel's supper on a tray. "Now, the couch folds out," she was saying. "And the linen's in the hall closet."

"I'll try your mother again from the Swansons'," said Marshall. "Their phone might be all right." He picked up his keys. The Swansons, it seemed, lived in the same building—in, according to Zena, a penthouse that had an incredible view. "Keep trying the line," he instructed Angel. "It might come on again at any time."

She looked up to see him opening the door for Zena. "Sure," she mumbled.

"We won't be too late," her father called as he vanished into the hall.

After they'd gone, she sat on the couch in the empty apartment. Once or twice she picked up the phone, but the line was still out. She needed to see someone who loved her; someone who wanted her around; someone who would never let her down, not in a billion years.

"You can stay out as late as you want," Angel said out loud, suddenly getting to her feet. "Because I'm not staying at all."

"You're joking, right? You're going on a *date? Now?*"

"For Pete's sake, Angel, I'm not going to the moon," Lindy pleaded. "I'll just be downstairs in the rec room."

Angel sat on the bed, staring at the back of her best friend's head. She couldn't get over it. She'd only just arrived, and already Lindy was planning to leave her. To spend the evening watching videos with some boy she'd met while he was serving her a slice of pizza at the mall!

"But it's storming! He'd not going to come over in this weather."

Lindy winked at her over her shoulder. "He's got a Jeep."

"Lindy . . ." She made an effort to keep her voice calm and reasonable. "How can you leave me alone now? Haven't you been listening to a word I said?"

"Of course I've been listening," Lindy said. She

216

glanced at Angel in the mirror as she started to put on her makeup. "And I think it's awful, what's happened. You know I do." She pulled at a loose eyelash. "But I didn't know you were coming, did I? It's taken me days to arrange this. I can't cancel now." She made up her face. "Or have you sitting on the sofa with us, can I?"

"But I'm your best friend," Angel reminded her. "And this is an emergency, Lindy. I have no money, and I can't get hold of my mom. . . . I can't stay with Dad and Zena. . . ."

Lindy added a little silver to the corners of her eyes. She stepped back to check the effect. "Don't get overwrought, Angel. Of course you're going to stay here. What sort of a best friend do you think I am? Stop being so childish. I'll be right downstairs. And you can watch TV or play music. Just make yourself at home." She smiled at herself in the mirror. "But this guy's important, too, Angel. You would not believe how gorgeous he is." She ran her tongue over her lips. "He's to die for. He's absolutely to die for."

Well, that's fortunate, Angel thought. *Because I really want to kill you.* How could Lindy, of all people, be abandoning her like this? Now, when Angel needed her most, when she had nowhere else to turn. Was this the girl who had said that nothing would ever come between them? That even if one of them married a man the other didn't like, they would still be best friends?

"Anyway," Lindy went on happily. "Jason has an eleven o'clock curfew on weekdays. I won't be that long."

217

Long? What did *long* mean? Ten minutes was long if you were listening to the principal drone on about the school dress code. But a day was nothing when you were lying on a beach.

Angel looked at the clock by Lindy's bed. It was seven. That meant four hours of making polite conversation with Mrs. Porterfield, who could only talk about bridge, home furnishings, and her cholesterol level. Or four hours of sitting by herself in Lindy's room, counting the minutes crawl by, while Lindy flirted with a gorgeous pizza man in the rec room. She'd rather be stuck in a lecture on skirt length or hair color. Of course, she could always go upstairs and talk to the maid. Maybe they could compare rooms.

"What do you think?" asked Lindy, spinning around. "I paid an absolute fortune for this dress. You should've heard my father when he found out how much it cost. I had to listen for a week to his lecture about all the poor people in the third world who don't even own a pair of shoes. But I just had to have it. I couldn't have lived without it."

Angel stared at the new dress. She used to think there were things she couldn't live without—a certain pair of shoes, a certain perfume, a new outfit every week. It wasn't true, though. That was something she'd been learning since she left Lisson Park. A person could live without expensive clothes and stuff like that, but not without people who cared about her.

Lindy spun once more. "You don't blame me, do you? You think it's great, don't you?"

In the past Angel had always humored Lindy. If

Lindy thought a boy was gorgeous and Angel thought he looked like something that had been thrown out of the reptilian gene pool, she had always said, "Well, he's not my type." If Lindy thought a blouse was the most beautiful item of clothing she'd ever seen and Angel thought it made her look like one of Mrs. Porterfield's armchairs, she had always said, "Well, it's not my style." She wasn't feeling so diplomatic now.

"I think you already have a dress like that," she snapped.

Lindy scowled. "No, I don't. The one you mean is blue, and the collar's different." She studied herself in the mirror again. "This one's much more *me*."

You mean there's not much to it, said the voice of B.J. Spatano in Angel's ear.

The doorbell rang.

Lindy didn't even glance at Angel as she raced to the door. "We'll talk later," she promised. "We'll stay up all night, like we used to." She came back to give Angel a hug. "Gosh, it's good to see you," she said. "It's just like old times, isn't it?"

Not quite, Angel thought as the doorbell rang again and Lindy fled from the room. *Not quite*.

Friendship and Lindy Porterfield might be fickle, Angel reasoned, *but true love lasts*. Friends might dump you to exchange saliva with a guy who sells pizza, but a boy who says he will love you till forever will love you till forever. That's what made love so special.

Angel trudged down the tasteful, tree-lined streets of Lisson Park, her bag over her shoulder, thinking

219

about love and how lucky it was that Gavin only lived a few blocks from Lindy. *If I had to go any farther, I'd collapse,* she told herself as she turned in at the Smythes' circular driveway. Her blood began to race. *He had to be home. Home waiting for me.* It wasn't easy to run when you were carrying an overstuffed carryall, but she did her best.

"Angel!" Gavin was so surprised he couldn't even smile. "Angel, what are you doing here?"

Her heart jumped at the sight of him, cool and handsome, standing in the doorway with his trenchcoat over his arm. Here, at last, was the person she could depend on. The person who cared. She smiled. "Aren't you going to ask me in?"

"Oh, sure, sure." Gavin stepped back. "It's just that . . . I . . ." He nodded toward the stairs. "I was just on my way out, that's all."

Unmindful of the Smythes' expensive carpet or the cashmere sweater and nervous expression worn by their only son, Angel dumped her wet bag on the floor and threw herself into Gavin's arms. "I wish I'd come here first," she whispered. "I wish I'd come straight to you."

"Angel, you're soaking wet!" He pulled away, brushing raindrops from his chest. "What did you do, walk here from Long Island?"

She took off her hat and shook out her hair. "Not quite," she said with a laugh. "But close." She laughed again, this time not quite so lightly. There was something about the way Gavin was looking at her. It made her think of the look of a person who has just discovered a beetle in his cornflakes. She pushed the thought away. It must be her, because she was so overwrought. Angel put on the sugar-sweet voice she only used with Gavin. "What's the matter?" she wheedled. "Aren't you glad to see me?"

"Of course I'm glad to see you." He smiled so she'd know he was glad. "I'm just surprised, that's all. I didn't— You didn't—"

"I thought you'd be happy to open your front door and find me on the porch," she said softly. Drawing nearer, she put her arms around his waist and rested her head on his shoulder. His arms encircled her.

"I just don't understand what you're doing here, that's all," Gavin said. "I thought . . . you're not . . . Angel, this is really a bad time. I have to be somewhere ten minutes ago."

She stood there for a few seconds, his arms around her like a ring of smoke. Why was it everyone had something more important to do than talk to her? Slowly, she released him, pulling back to study his face for the first time. It was not the face of a boy who is glad to see you. How had she convinced herself that it was? It was the face of a worm who has just spotted the fish swimming through the seaweed.

"Where?" she asked finally, surprised herself at how calm she sounded.

Gavin shifted from his left foot to his right. "Where?"

Maybe that was the thing about disappointment and rejection. Maybe after awhile you got used to it. It didn't matter anymore. She didn't even feel surprised that he wasn't glad to see her. More than that, she didn't really care. Looking at Gavin, she suddenly couldn't remember what it was about him that she'd found so attractive. He was just a good-looking boy who thought he was a gift from God and who was a pretty lousy kisser.

"Yes, where? If you're going out in this weather, you must know where." Her voice was losing its calm. "You're not just going to drive around with the top down in this storm, are you?"

Gavin's eyes focused on a point just beside her head and a few feet behind her. "Well . . . um . . . to tell the truth . . ." He drew a deep breath. "Well, to tell the truth, Angel, I'm going to see someone. It's sort of a date."

"A date?" It definitely looked as though everyone had managed to get along without her pretty well. Her tears of rage blurred Gavin's handsome face. "But you said you'd love me forever," she reminded him angrily. "You said there would never be anyone else like me."

"Well, yeah . . ." Gavin shrugged. "I mean, I know I said that, Angel, but you're hundreds of miles away now. I mean, you couldn't expect . . . I mean, face it Angel, life goes on."

"Forever" obviously wasn't as long as it used to be.

Gavin struggled on. "I mean, if you were here, it'd be different."

"But I am here," said Angel simply.

He shrugged again. "Yeah, well, . . . but you're not really here, are you?"

You're not really here. He was right, she wasn't really here. All at once, Angel wished that she weren't there at all. She wished she'd never left

Long Island. An urgent desire to be back in the old, cramped, and crumbling house on Bluff Drive took hold of her. Of all the things she never thought she'd feel this—a desire to be sitting at her desk in the attic, listening to the rain, while downstairs her mother worked out menus in the kitchen and Sean played Nintendo, and, a few feet away, B.J. Spatano lying with his feet up on her washed-silk bedspread, and his dog on his lap, flipping through her magazines and making stupid jokes. She missed her family. B.J. had been right. Denise and Sean were her family. They always had been. Even back in Lisson Park. Marshall was around for holidays and vacations and things like that, but the rest of the time he was working or busy somewhere. It was the three of them who had done things together: who trimmed the Christmas tree, and popped corn, and went out for ice-cream at eleven at night. Just as it was the three of them in Midville, sitting around talking, going shopping together, watching TV. *You're not really here.* B.J. had been right about that, too. You can't go back. Her mother was trying to build something new, but Angel had been holding onto the past. Holding onto Lisson Park. Holding onto Gavin and Lindy and her dad. Holding onto a home that wasn't hers anymore. Her home was on Bluff Drive, with Denise and Sean and an unquiet spirit with a big mouth.

"Why don't you stay here tonight?" Gavin asked, obviously relieved that the worst seemed to be over. "I'm sure my mother won't mind. We do have three guest rooms."

Angel watched his lips forming word after

word—*stay, mother, guest rooms*—but she didn't really care what he was saying. Her head was too filled with her own speeding thoughts.

Gavin picked up her bag. "Come on," he said. "I'll show you where you can stay."

But Angel was jamming her hat back on her head and buttoning her coat. She grabbed her carryall out of Gavin's hands. "No thanks," she said. "I have to get home."

"Okay," Denise said. "I'll call you as soon as I hear anything, and you do the same." She hung up the receiver and turned back to the room.

Sean couldn't remember when he'd seen her look so worried. "Well?" he asked. "What did Dad say?"

His mother sighed. "She was there, but he left her to visit some people he knows in the building. When he went down to check on her, she was gone." Denise took a tissue out of her pocket and blew her nose. "I blame myself," she said softly. "I know how headstrong and stubborn Angel is. . . . And I knew she was having a hard time."

Sean put an arm around her shoulders. "Try Lindy," he advised her. "And then try the drip."

Normally, this road was always busy. It was jammed with traffic in the day and bright with headlights all through the night. But not tonight. Tonight it had been taken over by the storm. Garbage cans rolled down the sidewalks, plastic bags flapped through the air like wings, broken branches smashed into the street. Tonight the road was deserted—deserted except for the occasional slow-moving car—and

Angel Lister, marching along with her head bent and the wind behind her.

She was going to walk home. It might take days— if this storm kept up, it might take years—but that's what she was going to do. She had no choice. A handful of change wasn't going to get her too far on the train, and she wasn't going back to her father's, or Gavin's, or Lindy's. She wanted to be home, back where she belonged. *You can make it,* she reassured herself as she struggled past a sign that suggested that she was heading in the right direction. *Just try not to drown or get run over by flying garbage.*

She was so busy just trying to walk that she was on top of it before she saw it. There, right in front of her, was something pink and green and silver. She felt like a sailor sighting the distant glimmer of a lighthouse on a storm-tossed night. She stared. She saw lights and people. She heard talk and music. A diner! A diner that was open! She could go inside and get a cup of coffee—she must at least have enough money for that. She could go in and have six cups of coffee, and maybe by then the rain would have died down a little. Angel Lister, the girl who had once sworn she would never eat in a place like this no matter how hungry she was, practically flew up the steps.

Angel held the menu up in front of her, and, as unobtrusively as she could, counted out the coins in her hand. She had just enough for a coffee and a doughnut. A coffee, a doughnut—and warmth, and a roof. *Who's not responsible? Who can't take care of herself?* An unfamiliar feeling of confidence and independence settled over her. She wasn't a little girl anymore: she was a woman of the world. A woman in charge of her own fate who took trains by herself and ate in diners and walked hundreds of miles in gale-force winds.

"What'll it be, honey?"

Angel looked up. A tired-looking, middle-aged woman in a soiled, green uniform was smiling at her, pencil poised.

Angel closed her hand around her money. "A cup of coffee and a chocolate doughnut."

The waitress raised an eyebrow. "That all?"

Angel's stomach growled. "Yes. That's all."

He was riding like he used to ride. Like he and the bike were one—moving together, thinking together, breathing together. Neither man nor machine, the old bike and him, but like a beast from some long-ago, untamed dream.

Hard and determined, B.J. rode against the wind. Against the wind and into the past. Every time he saw a shape across the divider, he expected to hear the wail of brakes, to see a set of headlights hurtling toward him, leaping through the air like a lion felling an antelope. His past. His nightmare. His death.

It had been a night like this. A night like this, on a road like this, racing down the shining black streak of highway, bending in the flash of headlights, listening to his own heart beating louder than the engine's roar. But he hadn't been on the Vincent. He'd gotten a ride into town with a friend of Danny's.

Guy had driven like a reindeer running out of hell.

B.J.'d tried to get Danny to go with him. "Why don't y'come and play pool with me and Mike and Tony?" But Danny and his friend had been in a hurry, chuckling to themselves. "Don't worry, man," Danny'd told him. "You go on, I'll see you soon." Mike, B.J., and Tony had been in the middle of a game when some guy had come in and started talking about all this money he was making. He must've been loaded, loaded or stupid, talking about all the money he was making for leaving the back door open to the liquor store where he worked. "Easy money," he'd kept saying. "Easy money. Nobody there now but the old man." And B.J. had known. He didn't even know how, but he'd known. He hadn't said anything to Mike, not a word. He'd just dropped his cue and held out his hand, and Mike had given him the keys to the Harley. "Just be careful," Mike had said. "Just watch out for yourself." "No sweat, man," B.J. had answered, thinking about Danny. "I'll be back inside an hour."

The miles fell behind as the rains poured and the wind yowled. B.J. hunched forward, every detail of that night as vivid as the moment he was in right now. Danny hadn't come back inside an hour. He hadn't seen B.J. soon. There'd been plenty to worry about. B.J. had reached the liquor store just in time to hear the gun go off. When he'd gotten inside, the other guy, Danny's friend, had passed him, running out the front, and Danny had been standing there, shaking as he stared at the body, the gun still in his hand. Only when B.J. had taken it from him had Danny run. He'd shoved B.J. out of the way and run into the parking lot, jumping into the blue Chevy as it tore away, the sound of sirens cutting through the night. But even then B.J. had still thought he could do something. He'd still thought he could save Danny. He'd been nuts. Nuts, and wilder than the night.

Just like he thought he could save Angel now. And just as wild.

Long after the waitress had disappeared behind the counter, Angel was still sitting there, looking down at the food she'd brought her—two doughnuts, a grilled cheese sandwich, and a cup of coffee—realizing how hungry she was. "Take it," the waitress had said when she'd protested that she hadn't ordered so much. "With this storm, we're only gonna end up throwing it out anyway." Angel couldn't decide where to start.

"Mind if I join you?"

She looked up, about to say no automatically. But the young man who had asked the question was already sliding into her booth.

"It's such a dreadful night," he was saying. "I don't feel like sitting on my own."

Angel was not in the habit of letting strange young men simply sit down with her and strike up a conversation. But it *was* a pretty dreadful night, and a lonely one as well. "I know what you mean," she said. She smiled back. And he was a pretty attractive young man. Much more attractive than Gavin, for instance. Older, too. More mature.

"Brandon," he said, extending his hand over the table. "Brandon King."

"Angel," she answered. "Angel Lister."

"Angel." His smile was a lot nicer than Gavin's, too. "What an appropriate name."

Brandon was explaining that he was on his way back to Columbia, where he was doing pre-law, when the waitress suddenly appeared beside him. He broke off in mid-sentence.

"What can I get you?" she asked, tapping her pencil against her pad. Her eyes went from Brandon to Angel and back again. Angel wasn't sure whether it was because they were both waitresses, but something in the woman's look made her think of her mother.

"Just coffee," said Brandon, waving her away. He leaned toward Angel. "Now, where was I?"

He was telling her all about his Porsche and how much it cost to keep it in a garage in New York when the waitress reappeared with his order. Again, she gave them that Denise Lister look. "Both checks," said Brandon, not looking up.

"What do you say?" he asked when he'd finished his coffee. "You're not really going to walk back to Long Island. And you can't stay in this dump all night. Look at the creeps who hang out here."

Angel looked. It wasn't exactly the Lisson Park Country Club.

He pushed his cup away. "Come to New York with me. You can be deejay. I've got a great sound system in the car."

The waitress dropped the checks on the table.

Angel hesitated, gazing into Brandon King's amazingly blue eyes. She knew that you weren't supposed to accept rides from strangers. Everyone knew that. But the kind of strangers you weren't supposed to accept rides from were not good-looking, well-dressed, pre-law students who drove Porsches. The kind of strangers you weren't supposed to accept rides from were hoods like B.J. Spatano.

"Okay," she said. "That'd be great."

This time the waitress looked only at Angel.

"She's not there, either?" asked Sean. He wished there was something he could say to stop his mother from looking so worried.

Denise turned from the phone and collapsed beside him on the sofa chair. "Nope," she said in a flat voice. "She's not with Lindy, and she's not at Gavin's." She jumped as a garbage can banged against a tree. The wind blowing off the water moaned around the back of the house. "She must be in the train station," she said, giving him a weak smile. "Probably nothing's moving because of the storm."

"Yeah, that's it," Sean agreed eagerly. "There aren't any trains, that's why she's not back yet."

"Maybe I should just call the police," said Denise, not meeting his eyes. "With this hurricane, or whatever it is, she might be stranded somewhere."

Sean moved closer. He knew he was forbidden to talk about the ghost, but this was an emergency. This was the one piece of news that could cheer his mother up. "You don't have to worry, Mom." He patted her arm. "B.J.'s gone after her. She'll be all right. He went on his bike."

Denise stared into Sean's glasses.

"Really," said Sean solemnly. "If anybody can find her, B.J. can."

230

"You mean this ghost of yours has special powers?" she said at last. She was almost smiling.

Sean shook his head. "No. I mean he's reliable."

It was the weirdest thing, but while Brandon was paying the bills, the waitress came back and tried to talk Angel out of going with him. What did she think she was, a guardian angel with a menu?

"Stay here," she said. "You can use the phone to call you mom."

How did the waitress know her mother didn't know where she was? Maybe there was something telepathic, connected, about waitresses. Like twins. It made Angel nervous, as though Denise were going to walk in the door at any second. Besides that, she couldn't hide her surprise that a waitress, in a diner, a person with ketchup stains on the pocket of her uniform, was trying to tell her what to do.

"It's all right," Angel replied stiffly. "I'm going with my friend."

Sitting in the plush warmth of the Porsche, looking through the CDs, laughing at Brandon's stories of life in the city, she couldn't help wondering if the waitress had been a little neurotic or something. Why should she want to stop her from going with Brandon? He was well-off, clean-cut, polite, and charming. Every mother's dream.

"Whew," he breathed, leaning closer to the windshield. "This storm is even worse now than it was before. I can't see a thing. We might as well be driving through water."

Angel slipped a new disk into the player. "Maybe we'll be able to drive out of it," she suggested. "You know, maybe it won't be so bad farther north."

"I really don't know if we're going to get much farther north." He shook his head thoughtfully. "I think we'd better consider stopping for the night. Do you have any money at all?"

Angel turned to look at him. That was not the kind of thing that a mother's dream said to young girls. "What?"

Brandon laughed. "I'm not trying to rob you, Angel. It's just that I'm short on cash. I only have enough for one room."

She stared out the window. The storm was bad, but it was passable. There were other cars on the road. Not many, maybe, but a few. If they drove slowly, if they stayed where it was well-lighted . . .

"But we don't have to stop. We just have to take it easy."

"You can take it easy if you want," said Brandon. "But not me. This car is brand-new. I don't want some tree to fall on it."

Don't be a little kid, Angel scolded herself. *Look at it from his point of view. It is an expensive car, and the rain is heavy. Just because he wants to stop somewhere, that doesn't mean he's going to try anything.*

Brandon glanced over at her. "Hey, you don't think that—" It was as though he were reading her mind. "You're not worried that I—" He laughed at the ridiculousness of the idea. "Angel, I am a gentleman and a scholar." He touched her hand. "Even if you are the prettiest girl I've seen in a long time."

Angel looked down at his hand on top of hers. Lindy would say yes. Rain as sharp as hailstones hit

232

the windows of the car. If Angel were to tell Lindy that she was thinking of getting out of a late-model Porsche to walk hundreds of miles in a hurricane rather than spend the night with one of the most eligible young men she'd ever met, Lindy would say she was crazy. She looked over at Brandon. He was smiling at her.

"You trust me, don't you?" He squeezed her hand. "You can, you know. I'm a nice guy." They started to slow down.

How did she know she could trust him? Because he said so? Lindy had told her that she would die without Angel. Her father had told her the divorce wouldn't change anything. Gavin had told her she was the only girl he would ever love.

"I'm going to get off this road at the next intersection, and we'll start looking for someplace to stay."

How come a jerk with a car like this don't have a credit card? asked a familiar voice in her head. *Tell me that, sweetheart. If he's so rich, how come he's broke?*

Angel was beginning to realize that there were people in the world who told you one thing when they really meant something else. She watched Brandon King as he shifted down for the light. It was very likely that he was one of those people.

The car stopped. Without really thinking, Angel grabbed her bag and jumped into the night.

"What are you, out of your mind, you little—" Brandon leaned over to grab for her, but she had the advantage of surprise. "Get back here!" he ordered. "You can't go anywhere in this."

233

She started walking as quickly as she could along the side of the road. The Porsche crawled beside her.

He rolled down the window. "You can't keep this up," he shouted as he followed her. "You're going to have to give up eventually and get back in the car."

Angel's heart was pounding. Out on the street the storm not only seemed worse, the world seemed abandoned. "No, I won't," she screamed back. "Just go on and leave me alone."

He laughed. It was a less pleasant sound than it had been before. "You wish," he said. "You're going to get in this car, and you're going to come with me, because you don't really have a choice."

The car cut in front of her and stopped. The emergency lights began to flash. Angel just stood there, watching the door open and Brandon King step into the storm. "Come on!" he shouted. "Don't be stupid. We'll go to a motel, and we'll have a nice time."

She took a step backward, suddenly feeling afraid. "Go away. I'm all right!"

"No, I won't go away. I feel responsible for you." He started toward her. "After all, I did offer you a lift."

She moved a little faster. He laughed. "You can't outrun me, honey. I'm a quarterback."

Just behind Brandon King, she could see the dim glow of an oncoming headlight. She would flag it down. She would make it stop, and Brandon would go away. She started hurrying toward the blur of light.

"Watch out!" screamed Brandon. "You'll get killed! Watch out!"

It happened so fast. One second she was standing on the shoulder of the road, and the next she was in the left-hand lane, frozen with terror. Once she gained the road she realized that she'd been crazy to think she could flag down the car. It was bearing down on her at an incredible speed. *It's a lunatic. A lunatic driving like a wild man. He can't stop. He's out of control.* She heard the slamming of the car door and a sharp sound as the Porsche pulled away, but all the while she just stood there, clutching her bag and waiting for her life to flash before her eyes. But all she could think was that she'd avoided being mauled only to be run over. *Well, I guess this will show them,* she thought. *They'll be sorry now.*

Blinded by the light, deafened by the sound of her own blood stampeding through her, Angel could think of only one thing to do. She closed her eyes and screamed.

B.J.

Suddenly the light swerved around her, and there he was, grinning from the side of the road.

"B.J.!"

"Need a ride?"

It was. It really was. William Joseph Spatano, looking wet and strong and safe. Looking like more than a friend.

Angel had never been so happy to see anyone in her life. She was so happy that she almost ran to him, wanting him to put his arms around her. So happy that she almost burst into tears.

He got off the bike. "What are y'gonna do? Stand there till someone else runs you down?"

235

And that was when she remembered what she was talking to. Mr. Take My Advice. Mr. I Told You So. How dare he follow her like she was some sort of baby, like she needed his help? How many times did she have to tell him that she didn't want him interfering in her life? How many times did she have to tell him to get lost? Who did he think he was?

She walked slowly to the bike with as much dignity as a girl who was soaked through, shaking with shock and hugging her bag like a life preserver, could be expected to manage.

"What are you doing here?" she demanded. At least her voice sounded nearly normal.

He held out his hands, palms up. "It's such a nice night, I figured I'd take a spin." He definitely had the most insolent smile she'd ever seen. "What were you doin'? Waitin' for a bus?"

"If you must know, I was on my way home," said Angel coolly. Rain dripped down her nose.

"And who was the geek in the Porsche? Your chauffeur?"

Already. He was starting already. He couldn't even wait till they got out of the storm. She'd never hear the end of this now. "I'm surprised you saw him, the speed you were going."

That, apparently, was funny.

He took a step toward her. "Sweetheart," he drawled, "just because I'm fast don't mean I'm not good."

This near to him, it was almost as though the storm had stopped, as though everything were all right. As though she could just fold herself into his arms. *Just take me out of here*, her heart was shouting.

Just take me home. She pulled herself together and told her heart to shut up. "Well, it's been nice talking to you," Angel said with a polite smile. "But I'm afraid I really have to get going now."

That was funny, too.

"Geez, you really are too much, y'know it?" He started taking off his jacket. "Here, put this on," he ordered. "You look like you've been drowned twice."

She shoved the jacket away. "I'm all right. I didn't need your help, you know. I can take care of myself."

"Oh, sure you can. That's why you were standin' in the middle of a major road in a storm with some creep tryin' to drag you into his car."

How could he be driving so fast and see so much? "You really are dense, aren't you? I was crossing the road. Pedestrians are supposed to walk facing oncoming traffic, or didn't they teach you that in reform school?"

He threw the jacket over her shoulders. "Facing oncoming traffic doesn't mean head-on, princess. You looked like a matador waiting for the bull." He winked. "A matador with a pink bag and a death wish."

"I really have to get going." She turned to walk away, but his hands were still on her and she couldn't seem to move.

"Put the jacket on right and get on the bike, Angel. Stop givin' me a hard time. I've had a rough night, and I'm not in the mood."

"On the *bike*? You expect me to ride on that suicide trap?"

He shook her, leaning his face into hers. "Will

237

you get real for a minute, sweetheart? It is raining. I rode hundreds of miles to find you—"

"No one asked you to. Don't start acting like some big hero."

"Hero?" He was shouting. "Well, maybe I'm no hero, Miss America, but you're a total jerk. You nearly got yourself killed and God knows what else—"

"And whose fault was that?" she screamed back. "What idiot nearly ran me down?"

He gave her a shove. "On," he commanded. "Just shut up for once in your life and get on the bike."

She held her ground. "You don't have helmets. It's illegal to ride without helmets."

"Not in 1959, it wasn't." He pushed her again.

She dug in her heels. "We'll be arrested."

"No, you won't. Jail's too good for you."

"I'd rather ride in a horse truck."

He was going to hit her. From the way his mouth and fists were clenched, she knew he was going to hit her. Instead, he gently touched his forehead against hers.

"Don't push me, Angel. If you don't get on the bike, I really will leave you here, and you can wait for your boyfriend in the fancy car to come back for you."

She wasn't sure whether she believed him or not. She looked into those eyes, but there was nothing to be seen.

Acting as though she were doing him a favor, she slowly slid her arms into the sleeves of the old jacket. It probably wasn't worth testing him to see if he really would leave her. He was nothing if not stubborn.

"And where am I supposed to sit, Mr. Genius? How am I supposed to hold on?"

He climbed on the bike. "You sit behind me, Miss Cheerleader. You hold on t'the seat."

"This is insane," she protested as she climbed on. "I can't ride with you. You're invisible."

He smiled at her over his shoulder. "Not tonight. Tonight everybody can see me. They'd never guess that you were sittin' behind a ghost." He winked. "I won't tell 'em, if you won't."

Angel groaned. "That's even worse. They'll think I'm a biker chick."

"They'll think you're pretty lucky, riding with me." He winked. "We'll go someplace where we can get out of this for awhile, and you can call your mom and fix up how you're gettin' back home."

She gripped the back of the seat. *If my friends could see me now,* she thought. Surprised, she realized that the friends she was thinking of weren't Gavin and Lindy.

"There's a diner up the road on the right," she said without thinking. "We could go there."

"Cool," said B.J. "I haven't been in a diner in years."

"You haven't been anywhere in years," said Angel.

"I know." B.J. kicked over the engine. "I had a nice, peaceful time before I met you."

Angel tightened her grip. "Are you sure this is a good idea?" she shouted as he turned the wheel. "I thought you said you don't ride in the rain."

"I don't," said B.J.

The old Vincent pulled out onto the road.

SAVE THE LAST DANCE FOR ME

DYAN SHELDON

How can someone who's dead seem so alive?

So what if B.J. saved Angel's life once before? He's still got a major attitude problem, and Angel wishes he'd act more like what he is, a dead guy, than the pain-in-the-neck big brother he seems to think he is. Worse than his constant snooping and dumb advice and rude remarks about the guys she's interested in, now B.J.'s beginning to act dopey about Angel's best friend, Suze.

What is it with him and Suze anyway? Angel knows B.J.'s nothing more than a cheap hood who died during a robbery attempt. But Suze thinks he's been misunderstood, a rebel and a loner who took the rap to protect someone else. Angel's happy enough to leave a decades-old mystery alone, but Suze has come up with the perfect incentive: if the girls find out the truth, maybe B.J.'s ghost can find peace at last—and stop bugging Angel.

0-8167-3794-0 • $3.95

Available wherever you buy books.